Cole shoved the door wide, gun drawn and ready. A string of fervent swears bit the air.

Before he could bark another order, Rita's eyes landed on a small black device near Cole's feet. Bright red numbers counted backward toward zero. The soft ticking of a clock registered with each change on the display.

17, 16, 15...

Rita gasped. "Is that a bomb?"

Papers fluttered through the air as Cole tossed the stack of folders from her hands toward the dock. He swung back to face her, this time gripping her wrists and tugging her up the steps toward him.

Rita's feet bumbled forward, catching each rung on autopilot while she stared, transfixed by the device that would end her too-short life.

9, 8, 7...

He yanked her arms, dragging her away from the device when she landed on deck beside it, but her body didn't respond.

"Rita!" Cole yelled, his voice thick with demand and authority.

6, 5, 4...

SHADOW POINT DEPUTY

Julie Anne Lindsey

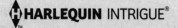

Dedicated to cat ladies. You are my people.

ISBN-13: 978-1-335-60414-9

Shadow Point Deputy

Copyright © 2018 by Julie Anne Lindsey

Recycling programs
for this product may
not exist in your area.

Printed in U.S.A.

™ www.Harlequin.com

Julie Anne Lindsey is a multi-genre author who writes the stories that keep her up at night. She's a self-proclaimed nerd with a penchant for words and proclivity for fun. Julie lives in rural Ohio with her husband and three small children. Today, she hopes to make someone smile. One day she plans to change the world. Julie is a member of the International Thriller Writers and Sisters in Crime. Learn more about Julie Anne Lindsey at julieannelindsey.com.

Books by Julie Anne Lindsey

Harlequin Intrigue

Visit the Author Profile page at Harlequin.com.

CAST OF CHARACTERS

Rita Horn—When Rita stops by the abandoned docks to feed the homeless cats on her way home from work, she accidentally stumbles onto a murder in progress. Now she's running for her life from a killer determined to leave no witnesses alive.

Cole Garrett—The youngest of the Garrett brothers and a Cade County deputy, Cole will do whatever it takes to catch the killer and protect the woman who is fast stealing his heart.

West Garrett—Cade County sheriff willing to do whatever it takes to support his brother, catch the killer and protect his hometown.

Blake Garrett—FBI agent and eldest Garrett brother. Blake's no-nonsense approach to hunting criminals puts him shoulder to shoulder with his younger brothers, determined to defend Rita and put the bad guy behind bars.

Ryan Horn—Rita's younger brother, a college student inadvertently pulled into the danger his sister stumbled upon.

Deputy Lomar—Cade County deputy, dedicated lawman and friend to the Garrett family. He stands by Cole and West as they race to find the man who is threatening Rita's life and nearly took her brother's.

Chapter One

Rita Horn parked her new pickup truck in the muddy gravel lot across from the docks. She dragged a bag of dry kibble from the bed and squinted at a dozen feline silhouettes framed by the sunset. It was a shame so many cats were homeless in Shadow Point. She'd take them all in if she could, but the three she already had were sure to protest.

"Here, kitty, kitty," she called, shivering against the brisk autumn breeze. Feeding the strays seemed a decent compromise to adopting them all, but it didn't minimize the guilt she experienced every time she stopped to check on them. If they had to be on their own, she supposed the abandoned factories along the waterfront made a decent haven. There was camaraderie, no natural predators and plenty of mice to sustain them when Rita worked late and missed her usual stop.

The cats swarmed her ankles as she rounded the building's edge, mewling and climbing over one another to get to the food. She stopped at a line of cement bowls she'd purchased from a local landscaper when the pet store versions had insisted on blowing away.

"Who's hungry?" She tipped the bag over the bowls, filling each to its rim. "Ah-ah-ah." She nudged a growling pair apart. "No fighting. There's plenty for everyone."

The bag was nearly empty when a latecomer trotted into view. The little orange-and-white tabby had something smeared over its face and down one side.

"What is that?" Rita crouched for a closer look. Deep crimson streaks flattened the kitty's fur into matted stripes. Rita clutched her chest. "My poor baby. What happened to you?" She reached for the tabby, but he jumped free with a hiss. It was easy to forget many of the cats were feral, not abandoned. It had taken weeks to get some to come out and see her at dinnertime. She clucked her tongue and extended a hand with the last of the kibble on her palm. The little guy wouldn't survive long with an injury that had bled so much. He needed the wound cleaned, antibiotics and probably stitches.

"Kitty," she cooed. The injured cat darted away, and Rita dashed after him, leaving the empty bag behind.

"Kitty, kitty, kitty." Her sensible three-inch heels clicked and snapped against the cold ground as she gave chase. She stopped short at a fence marked NO TRESPASSING. The cat paused a moment beyond the chain-link barrier before screeching out of sight.

"Darn it." She dropped the kibble from her palm and scanned the scene, debating the importance of her flawless, law-abiding record when that kitty needed a doctor.

A line of bloody paw prints knotted her tummy and propelled her to action. If she was caught, at least she could give a good explanation. Surely no one would fault a woman for trying to help an injured animal.

Rita shored up her nerve and tugged the gate where a thick chain and padlock held it loosely to the fence. There was enough space to slip inside if she held the gate and ducked beneath the chain, so she took a deep breath and went in. She followed the trail around the factory's edge, admiring the soft cotton candy glow of a setting sun as it gave way to twilight. The cat stared down at her from a windowsill eight feet in the air. "Are you even hurt?"

She scanned the scene for another injured animal. Where had the blood come from, if not from the cat who was wearing it? A dark puddle drew her forward, toward a narrow object several yards away. The air seemed to sizzle with danger as she scooped an expensive-looking pen off the ground. An odd thing to find at an abandoned factory, unless developers had been here. Maybe the state was finally going to make good on the promise to renovate the area. She froze as the tip of her shoe slid against the slick cement and swallowed a scream when the puddle came clearly into view, red as the sun burning its last rays of daylight off the water.

Rita raked her cell phone from a coat pocket with trembling fingers. There was far too much blood to have come from a cat.

A sudden splash sent ice fingers down her spine, and the low murmur of voices pushed her back to the building's edge. She closed her eyes to summon a thread of bravery, then peeked toward the sounds with caution.

The angle of the sunset reduced both figures to faceless silhouettes. They were clearly male with broad shoulders and strong gaits, but they were of strikingly different heights. Together, they strode beneath a cone of security light, revealing one man's dress shirt and the other's official-looking jacket, complete with patches she couldn't read from that distance. Rita's heart took off at a sprint as a dark stain down the front of the dress shirt began to look a lot like the puddle she'd just seen. The man with the stained shirt wiped his hands on a rag. A gun holster nestled safely against his side.

A black sedan seemed to manifest from the shadows, parked silently beside a line of blue barrels. The trunk popped open as the men approached, revealing what appeared to be more blood and a number of firearms. The man tossed the rag into the trunk, then dragged a suit jacket out. He threaded his arms through the sleeves and fastened two buttons over the broad crimson stain.

Rita swiped her phone screen to life. The little device rocked unsteadily in her sweat-slicked palm. Her breaths shortened and her heart rate spiked uncomfortably. There wasn't enough air, and she couldn't swallow. Rita gripped her phone tighter and fought the wave of panic quickly taking control. Not since she lost her mother had anxiety come on so quickly.

She pressed her back to the wall and returned the phone to her pocket. She needed to sit down before she fell over. Her eyelids slid shut for an internal pep talk, and she reopened them with purpose. She'd make the call from someplace safe. Someplace she could breathe. She forced the last ounce of bravery from her bones and tiptoed back through the shadows, along the building's edge, careful not to let her heels smack against the ground.

The snick of a closing trunk and soft purr of an engine were behind her. A set of low growls rose before her near the food bowls. Rita's muscles tensed. *No fighting*, she prayed. *Not now.*

The sound grew steadily into the familiar squawks of a feline brawl. A beam of light flashed over the ground before her, sweeping and narrowing as it drew nearer.

"Who's there?" The man in the official-looking jacket moved in her direction. The familiar Cade County Sheriff's Department logo was on his chest.

That could not be good.

Rita burst into motion, running as quickly as her trembling legs would carry her toward her truck, through the chained gate and across the gravel lot.

"Stop!" the man's voice boomed behind her, punctuated by the echoes of heavy footfalls.

Not today, officer, she thought as she dived behind the wheel. Something bad had definitely happened at the docks tonight. She didn't know what, and she wasn't about to become another puddle on the concrete.

Chapter Two

Rain poured over Deputy Cole Garrett's hat and slicker. Heavy storm clouds had masked the sunrise, but Shadow Point was still in motion. The blue-collar town had risen with the sun for a hundred years. Farmers. Bus drivers. Factory workers. Somehow the body pulled from the river wore a watch worth more than Cole's first truck.

He peered through the downpour at his older brother and current Cade County sheriff, West Garrett. "Recognize him?"

West's frown deepened. "Nope."

Dressed like he was, no one probably would. Folks with that kind of money drove right on through Shadow Point. "Maybe he was visiting family," Cole suggested, "or was here on business."

West shot Cole a look. "By the looks of the bullet hole in his forehead, business wasn't good."

Members of the local coroner's office loaded the waterlogged body onto a gurney and covered it with a white sheet. The medical examiner presented West with a clipboard. "We'll do our preliminaries and get back with you."

West followed the coroner back to the van.

Cole flashed his light over the scene, seeking anything that might explain how a stranger wound up murdered and floating in the water before dawn. The river had surely stripped the body of any clues, but maybe the killer had left footprints or the shell casing on land.

He moved methodically upriver, toward a set of abandoned factories by the docks. The shielded space seemed a more likely location for an execution than the sodden, unobstructed field where the body had been pushed ashore.

He returned the flashlight to his belt as the storm peeled back its efforts. A swarm of cats came into view near the largest building, gathered beneath a broad metal awning. They cried at the sight of him, and Cole changed trajectories, drawn to the mass of complaining felines.

The coroner's van motored away in the distance, rounding a bend and drifting out of sight. West's cruiser rolled quietly into a muddy gravel lot near the factory.

The world grew brighter by the second, finally relieved of the relentless storm.

"A bit off the path, aren't you?" West called, slamming the door behind him.

Cole stared at a line of cement bowls and a shredded cat food bag. "I don't think so." He nudged the soggy paper with his toe. "Someone fed the cats. Wasn't the first time, either. They didn't scatter when they saw me."

West cast a glance at the crowd of furry spectators, then turned his attention to the cruiser. "There were some tire tracks where I parked. They're washed out. Tread marks are gone."

"Let's measure them," Cole suggested. "Could be something. Might be how they brought the body here." Cole moved toward the cats, shooing them and scrutinizing the only patch of dry ground for miles.

"West." A set of bloody paw prints and the pointy outline of one shoe appeared beneath a broad awning. A white slip of paper clung to the sheet-metal door. A receipt dated the night before. The rest of the print was blurred away but he was certain it said cat food. "We've got a witness out there somewhere."

RITA STARED AT the clock above her fireplace and debated leaving for work an hour early. She'd been dressed since dawn, having given up on sleep hours before. The raging storm had rattled her windows and her mind. Each time her lids had grown heavy, she imagined the man from the docks trying to break down the door, only to wake again with the realization it was just the wind.

The same carousel of questions ran endlessly around her mind. What had she really seen? What sort of thing would involve so much blood, the docks and the local sheriff's department? Did the man giving chase recognize her? If so, what would happen next?

She'd watched the news on the edge of her seat, waiting for reports of whatever had happened at the docks, but there were none. Nothing in the morning paper, either.

A sharp pounding on the front door nearly sent her out the back. She inched across the living room and peeked through the curtains. Her little brother, Ryan, stood on the porch rubbing his palms together and puffing into his hands. The temperature must've dropped after she'd left the docks.

She opened the door with a forced smile, then jerked him inside. "Hey, what are you doing here?" She secured the door behind him and flipped the lock, hoping to look more normal than she felt.

He dragged his gaze from the locked door to her. "You said I could borrow your truck. My new roommate is moving in." He tented his dark brows, green eyes flashing in suspicion. "Are you okay?"

Ryan was nineteen and a sophomore at the university one town over. He was a full seven years her junior, with a misplaced big brother attitude. She'd helped raise him, and not the other way around.

"Yep." She tugged her ear and hefted a passing cat into her arms. The sight of her feline family usually brought her great comfort, but today they only delivered flashbacks of the docks.

"I thought you didn't have to be at work for an hour," Ryan said.

"I don't."

He scanned her freshly straightened living room, the result of too much time and anxiety with zero sleep. "Since when are you up and dressed by now, and why is your place so clean? What's going on?"

Rita's cheeks ached from the forced congeniality. What she wanted to do was cry. "Nothing." She dropped the act and pinched the bridge of her nose with one hand while cradling her kitty with the other. "I had trouble sleeping. Can I get you some coffee? Are you hungry?" Her gaze jumped again to the hands of the clock that never seemed to move. Going to work early wasn't a bad thing. It was normal, really. Not for her, but lots of other people did it. Maybe she could finally make some headway with the files on her desk, and the distraction would keep her mind off the slew of questions that she had no way of answering.

Ryan's hand danced before her. A US Army key ring swung from one finger. "Did you hear anything I just said?"

"What?"

He cocked a hip and dropped his arm. "Did someone hurt you?"

"No. Of course not." That was funny. Self-defense was a mandatory course of education in the Horn family, had been even before they'd lost their mother. Though no amount of self-defense training could've saved her from the drunk driver who'd taken her from them.

Rita dropped the cat on the couch. "Let me grab my purse." Her breath caught as she pulled back the zipper, revealing the pen she'd found at the docks inside. She'd considered throwing it away when she found it in her coat pocket, but decided to keep it until she knew what had happened. Maybe it was evidence.

"Give me one more minute," she called into the living room.

Rita grabbed a sandwich bag from the lazy Susan and wrapped the pen in tissues before stuffing it inside. If being trampled by thirty cats at an abandoned dock wasn't contamination enough, one night in her disaster of a handbag had surely ruined the pen's chances of being useful. But with technology these days, maybe someone could do something with it. If only she knew who to give it to or if she should. She rubbed her forehead and swallowed a lump of emotion. Was it evidence? Was she crazy? Maybe both. She sealed the bag and stuffed it back into her purse.

"Found it." She dropped the bag on the couch beside her white Himalayan rescue. The other two cats leaped onto the sofa and stuck their noses into her bag.

She presented the key to her new truck on one palm. "Take care of my baby."

He made the trade with enthusiasm, dropping the key to his twenty-year-old yellow hatchback into her newly empty hand. "And you take care of Suzie Sunshine."

Rita snorted and dragged one finger in a small X shape over her heart. "Do you need money for gas or lunch? How are your grades?"

Ryan backed toward the door. "I'm good. Grades are fine. I am meeting the guys for a cram session, though. So I should get going. I've got two morning exams. All those professors want me to learn things." He pretended to choke himself.

Rita clapped slowly, and a genuine smile formed on her lips. "The future of America, ladies and gentlemen." Education had always been high on Rita's priority list, but never on Ryan's. It had been all she could do to convince him to get a degree before enlisting in the army alongside their father. With a degree he could at least enter the service as an officer and be prepared for a career afterward.

He turned for the door.

"Wait." Rita pried the pile of cats from her handbag and set them aside. "I'll walk you out." She stroked the kitties' heads and scratched their chins. "Try to behave."

A thick fog had settled in after the night's heavy rains, making it impossible to see the stop sign at the end of the block and adding a Hitchcockian feel to her already pear-shaped world.

Ryan angled her silver Ford smoothly out of the driveway.

She coaxed his rusty hatchback to life. The stench of exhaust bit her nose and the air.

Ten minutes later, she set her purse on the municipal building's security scanner and nodded at the guards. She collected her things on the other side and walked quickly away, feeling irrationally conspicuous, knowing the pen lay inside.

Her heels snapped and cracked against polished marble as she crossed the cavernous foyer and climbed the wide, sweeping staircase. Cade County wasn't small, but it was rural, and the population was low, making one grand building a sufficient hub for the courthouse and local government offices, including hers at the County Treasurer. Oil paintings of the governor, senator and US presidents lined the second-floor hallways.

Rita ducked into her office and dropped onto her rolling chair with determination. Once she cleared the clutter from her head and desk, she'd give the sheriff's department a call. Anonymously. She'd been trespassing, after all, and she wouldn't be in this predicament if she'd obeyed the law and heeded the sign. She dropped her head into waiting palms. What would she say? She suspected that something bad happened? The storm had surely erased any evidence, and hadn't a deputy been there last night?

Why, yes. He had. And she'd *run* from him. A groan escaped her lips.

"Good morning, Rita!" A perky voice split the silence.

Rita jerked upright. "Hello."

The receptionist stared expectantly. "You're here bright and early." She fluffed giant blond hair and straightened a spray of stiff bangs.

"Hoping to catch up." Rita motioned to the pile of folders on her desk.

"Any luck?"

"Not really." She shouldn't have come in today. The office didn't feel like a distraction. It felt like a prison. "I think I'm going to make a coffee run before I get started." Maybe a little fresh air would help. "Can I get you something?"

The woman raised her steaming mug higher. "Kinda got that covered."

"Right. Sorry." Rita grabbed her coat and purse. "I won't be long." She straightened her white silk blouse and black pencil skirt, then hustled downstairs, taking the side exit into a public garden to catch her breath.

A slight drizzle forced her to stay near the door, where a small overhang served as shelter. The benches were wet. The ground waterlogged. Narrow puddles filled the spaces between walkway paving stones. She inhaled the cool, misty air and shook her hands out at the wrists. She didn't need fresh air or caffeine. She needed answers, and the only way she'd get them was to call the police like she should have done last night. It was better to report something that turned out to be nothing than to not speak up and find out later that her call could have helped someone.

She marched back inside with resolve and climbed the stairs to her office. Her steps slowed at the sight of a deputy speaking with the receptionist inside her glass office doors. If she truly planned to report what she'd seen, this was the time, but her muscles seemed to atrophy at the thought. There was something unsettling about his stance. She hadn't seen the faces of the men at the docks, but this deputy seemed familiar in a way that raised the hair on her arms.

She slipped into an alcove and waited. When the deputy reappeared on the steps to the building's front doors, she dialed the main line to the receptionist.

"Cade County Treasurer. This is Cyndi."

"Hi, Cyndi, this is Rita."

"Rita? Talk about timing! A deputy sheriff was just in here looking for you. Did he find you? I told him you went for coffee. Probably at that diner around the corner. Is that where you went?"

A cold sweat broke over Rita's brow. "Yes. Did he say what he wanted?"

"No. Only that he'd hoped to catch you."

"Did you get his name?"

Cyndi paused. "No. Honey, are you in some kind of trouble?"

Rita moved double time down the rear staircase. "No. Not at all. I'm feeling sick, though. I think that's why I was so distracted earlier. It's really hitting me now."

"Oh, well, then you should go home. I can't afford to get sick. Remember when I got that stomach flu last spring?"

How could she forget? Anytime anyone complained about so much as a headache in Cyndi's presence, they were reminded of her personal near-death experience in March. "Mmm-hmm. You know what? I think I have that."

"Oh, dear."

"Yep. I'm going to head home. Rest." Rita jogged through the door and across the employee lot toward Ryan's decrepit compact. "Cyndi? I've got to go. I think I'm going to be sick."

"You need lots of fluids."

"Okay." She dropped behind the steering wheel and gunned the little engine to life. What she really needed was to go home and pull herself together. "Thank you. Goodbye."

The phone rang in her hand, and she tossed it aside. The only person she'd answer for today was Ryan, and that wasn't his number. Everyone else could get in line.

She made a bunch of paranoid and probably unnecessary turns before arriving on her street almost twenty minutes later. Several neighbors stood on her lawn beside a cruiser in the driveway. Fear and panic bubbled in her core.

She cranked Ryan's window down and hooked an elbow over the frame. "Mrs. Wilcox," she stage-whispered. An elderly woman turned to face her. The woman hustled in her direction.

"What's going on?" Rita asked, sinking low in the driver's seat. Her tummy bubbled with anxiety at the sight of a cruiser at her home.

"Betty was jogging past and saw the cats in your yard." She pointed to a woman in hot pink running gear and a matching sun visor. "She recognized them because they spend so much time in your window."

"My cats were outside?" Rita gasped. "Are they okay?"

"Well, yes," she said, glancing back at Rita's home. "Betty collected the little lovebugs, then knocked on your door and it opened. The whole place was a mess, so she dropped them inside, pulled the door shut, then came to me, and I called the cops."

A rock formed in Rita's throat. "My house is a mess?" she croaked.

The older woman bobbed her head. "Trashed. The deputy was here in minutes. Must've been in the area."

Her heart hammered and her pulse beat in her ears. Someone had been in her home.

And a deputy was in there now.

Chapter Three

Cole had gritted his teeth and dragged his heels when the call came in from Dispatch about a possible B and E on Maple. Leaving West alone with an active murder investigation seemed irresponsible, but one of the problems in a department with only six deputies was coverage. The next man's shift wouldn't start for two hours unless West called him in sooner. Meanwhile, the homeowner on Maple had left work early and wasn't answering her phone. Cole had reluctantly made the trip to check on things.

The front door was unlocked with no signs of tampering, but the place had been destroyed. The neighbors hadn't seen or heard anything out of the ordinary, but every item in sight was upended, overturned or partially disassembled. Bookshelves were emptied. Drawers were dumped. Yet the television and computer were completely untouched.

Not a very effective robbery. So why break in? And where was the homeowner? He double-checked the name on his notepad. Rita Horn. Maybe this was revenge. Something personal. Maybe the work of a jaded ex or wronged family member.

Whatever it was, it was weird.

He scrubbed a palm over his face. First a body had turned up in the river, and now there was a break-in east of the railroad tracks. In a neighborhood known for its distinct lack of crimes. His exhale was long and slow. What was going on with this day?

The tip of his boot nicked a fallen photograph, and he pulled the thick white frame off the floor. "Well, what do you know?" He grinned. He'd recognize those smart hazel eyes anywhere.

The jaw-dropping redhead worked at the municipal building. He'd taken notice of her last fall while delivering a criminal to court through the rear alley entrance. She'd been handing out homemade sandwiches and bottled water to a throng of homeless people at lunchtime. Her floral wrap dress and high heels had been a stunning contrast to the dirty and disheveled men and women in her care. If memory served him, she'd called several of the people by their names.

He set the frame on the fireplace mantel, feeling much better about leaving West at the docks.

"Here she is!" A voice called from the lawn. "She's okay!"

Cole turned on his heel and went to save the day.

"Miss Horn?" He strode in the direction of a rusty yellow car. "I'm Deputy Cole Garrett. Can you please park your vehicle?"

She nodded behind the driver's-side window.

Her white-knuckle grip and wide eyes worried him.

Current circumstances aside, Rita was the poster child for calm and centered. He'd started noticing her every time he made a trip to the courts after that day in the alley. Unfortunately, they'd never made eye contact, and unlike most women in town, she didn't seem to know he existed.

The car rolled slowly to the curb and idled several moments before the engine settled.

She got out, closed the door and moved cautiously in Cole's direction. "What's going on?" Her gaze darted nervously over the scene, catching on his cruiser, then the patch on his jacket.

A gray-haired woman popped up at her side. "I was scared when you didn't answer the phone. Your office said you'd left, but you didn't answer."

"I'm sorry, Doris." Rita soothed the elderly woman. "I wasn't feeling well. I'm not myself today."

"I just thank my stars you weren't home when this happened," Doris said.

"What happened, exactly?" Rita asked again, moving her attention to Cole.

"Your neighbors reported a possible break-in about thirty minutes ago. When did you say you left the municipal building?"

Her eyes narrowed. "How do you know I was at the municipal building?"

Cole put on his most charming smile, hoping to soothe the sudden alarm in her tone. "I've seen you there."

Her cheeks darkened, but she didn't comment.

It was none of his business, but Rita Horn didn't look

sick. In fact, she looked fantastic. Her skirt and blouse fit in all the right places, accentuating her curves without giving away the details.

Man, he would love to know her details.

She crossed her arms over her chest, drawing the silky material of her blouse tighter.

Dear Lord.

"I went in early."

Cole swept a hand toward her front door and forced his gaze there, as well. "Would you like to see if anything is missing?" He moved onto the stoop, hoping she'd follow. Honestly, she looked like she might get back in her car and flee. "Any chance you forgot to lock the door this morning?"

"No." Her sweet voice sounded behind him. "I even double-checked the knob."

He angled himself for a look at her. "Do you always double-check or was something different today?"

She pursed her lips.

Cole imagined kissing them apart.

He leaned against the handrail to her porch, allowing her to pass. "I can't help thinking about the fact there hasn't been trouble like this in your neighborhood for quite some time, and it happened on a day when you got sick and left work early. Also on a day you felt compelled to double-check your lock."

"Maybe you're reading too much into this."

He shrugged. "That's possible. It's certainly a side effect of the job."

Rita slid past him into her home, and a zip of electricity snapped over his skin. "Can you think of anyone who might've done something like this, Miss Horn?"

She swept long auburn locks over her shoulder and bundled the strands in one fist. "No." She lowered her arms to lock around her middle. "You can call me Rita."

COLE UNZIPPED THE black duffel he'd left by the door.

"What are you doing?" The fear in her voice startled him.

He raised his palms in a show of innocence. "I'm going to dust the knob and jamb for fingerprints. Maybe replace this old dead bolt."

She lifted a finger. "Can I see what's in the bag?"

Cole felt his forehead pucker as he stretched the duffel wide for her inspection.

"Okay." Her face flushed with the words. "I don't use the dead bolt. It sticks."

"Care if I put the new one on before I go? It won't stop a professional from getting inside, but it'll slow one down, and in this neighborhood, time is your friend. I have a feeling those people on your lawn don't miss much."

Her lips turned down slightly. "You just happen to have a spare dead bolt with you?"

"No. I've been planning to change mine for months but haven't gotten around to it."

She seemed to mull that over. "Can you leave the door open while you work?"

"Sure." He applied the dusting powder to her knob and jamb. "You sure you can't think of anyone who'd want to get in here?"

"Like who?" Rita lifted a fancy pillow from the floor and clutched it to her chest.

Cole split his attention between her and his work. "I don't know. Maybe a rival or an ex. Maybe a lover's significant other?"

Her shocked expression turned to disgust. "That's awful." She dropped the pillow onto her couch and lined it up with the others. Delicate stitching over a tiny yellow flower formed the words *Suck it up Buttercup.*

Cole smiled.

She frowned. "I don't have any rivals or lunatic exes, and I certainly don't get involved with men who have significant others." She threw his final words back at him. "What kind of women do you normally deal with, Deputy Garrett?"

He smiled at the pleasant sound of his name on her tongue. "You can call me Cole." He stretched to his feet and extended a hand her way.

She eyeballed his hand. "I recognize you from the courthouse."

A smile spread over his lips. "Is that right?"

Rita blushed and slid her thin hand into his. "Can I make you some coffee?"

"That'd be nice." He turned back to the door with a rush of satisfaction.

Rita righted furniture and photos while Cole finished his work on her door and the coffee brewed. The small, inviting space was magazine perfect when he packed up his things. The overall result was very sexy librarian. Claw-footed furniture, books by the boatload and more fancy pillows with goofy sayings like *Hot Mess, Sassy*, and *Hell to the No*.

Cole shook his head. "You might want to think about getting a new knob, too. Maybe something with a code."

"Sure." She rolled the vacuum into view, then wiped a bead of sweat from her brow. "Coffee should be ready."

"Care if I shut the door and test the lock?"

"No. It's fine." She returned a moment later with two fragile-looking cups and set them on the coffee table. "Do you take cream or sugar?"

Cole laughed. "No, but thanks." He made a show of testing the door's integrity and admiring his personal handyman skills. "I think this is all set. I'll let you know about the prints." He dropped the keys to her new dead bolt on the table, then helped himself to a seat in the narrow armchair. "You live here alone?"

"Yeah. For a couple years since Ryan moved out."

Cole felt his jaw lock. "Ryan?" Maybe there was an angry ex out there somewhere who needed a swift kick in the ass. Cole adjusted his position in the little seat and hiked one foot onto the opposite leg. The idea of a man attempting to harm or frighten Rita set his teeth on edge.

"He's my little brother." She flipped the lid on a scrapbook beside his coffee. "There."

A younger, masculine version of Rita centered every photo. Ryan was tall and gangly, like Cole used to be. At least eight inches taller than his big sister, who was tucked beneath his arm in many of the pictures. "You're close. That's nice. My family's like that. Painfully so."

She smiled.

"Did you say Ryan lived here?"

"Yeah. Until he moved into a dorm for freshman year. I was his legal guardian through high school." Deep sadness swam in her hazel eyes.

Cole found himself leaning forward, suddenly eager to understand her burdens and lighten them.

"Our mother was hit by a drunk driver in Oklahoma. Ryan came to live with me after the funeral."

"I'm sorry. I had no idea." He couldn't imagine losing a parent. Especially not in high school. And he surely couldn't have raised a teenager when he was in his twenties. "Your dad's not in the picture?"

She rolled her eyes and traced the gilded rim of her dainty cup with a fingertip. "No. He's in Kuwait or Afghanistan or somewhere else where people need him." There was no mistaking the disappointment in her tone. She set her cup aside and slid her palms up and down her thighs, then folded her fingers on her lap.

"Do I make you nervous?"

She looked at her feet. "No. Your presence is extremely comforting, actually, but I've had a long morning."

"And you don't feel well," he reminded her.

"Right."

"Anything you want to talk about?" he prompted.

Rita pressed her lips into a white line and shook her head.

He levered himself off the chair and went to fish a card from his bag, leaving his finished coffee where it stood. There was little left for him to do if she wasn't talking, and West could use his help back at the docks.

She followed Cole to the door and opened it for him. Soft scents of vanilla and honey lifted from her skin and hair.

Cole scribbled his cell number across the back of his card. "If you need anything else or think of something you want to tell me, give me a call. I always answer, and I can be here quick. Meanwhile, I'll add your street to the other deputies' patrol routes."

"No. Don't." Rita's hand flashed up from her side, and curled around his wrist.

He waited for additional information that didn't come. "That's it? Just don't?"

Her home had been ransacked, but she didn't want to know the sheriff's department was keeping watch?

Her face went slack as she released him. "I'm fine. There's no need to send anyone else out. Thank you for coming." She practically shoved him across the threshold, then cranked the new lock behind him.

Cole dropped behind the wheel of his cruiser and grabbed the radio to call in his whereabouts before shifting into gear.

In the distance, a high-end sedan pulled away from the curb and took an immediate turn out of sight. Cole set the radio aside and reversed down the drive. He hadn't noticed the car when he went outside to walk Rita in, and it hadn't been there while he'd worked on her open door. Maybe it was nothing, or his attraction to Rita making him crazy, but something told him he'd better follow that car.

RITA WATCHED FROM her window as the handsome deputy pulled away. Cole Garrett wasn't the man from the docks and her office. She'd have recognized Cole anywhere. He was the one who settled fistfights outside the courtrooms and calmed criminals being loaded into vehicles destined for prison, and the one on his knees beside benches where folks cried over an unfair verdict. Cole Garrett was a peacekeeper and a hero.

When the coast was clear, Rita kicked off her heels and traded her pencil skirt for a pair of blue jeans. She stuffed bare feet into white, laceless sneakers and grabbed her laptop bag and purse.

Five minutes later, she parked Ryan's car against the curb outside a crowded café and wandered inside. On television, people being hunted always went somewhere with witnesses. The café seemed a smart choice. Even if she wasn't being hunted, it surely felt that way, and her home was too quiet. Too vulnerable. If someone got inside while she was there alone, the invader would have complete privacy to do anything he wanted.

Her stomach protested the thought. "A bottle of water, please," she said to the barista.

"Three dollars." He set her order on the counter.

Rita gave him a five and walked away. She chose a tall table near the back of the brightly lit room and climbed onto a seat with a view of the front door and window, and also of the muted television anchored near the ceiling. She should've told Cole her story. She had to trust someone, and every cell in her body said she could unequivocally trust him. It was stupid that she hadn't. She dug his card from her bag and set it on the table. She needed to stop feeling overwhelmed and start figuring this mess out.

What would she say? Where should she begin?

The white noise of two dozen voices soothed her frayed nerves. She rubbed cold fingertips in small circles against her temples, plotting ways to open the disturbing conversation. *Hello, this is Rita Horn. I know we've only just met, but I wanted you to know that I think one of the other deputies is a murderer.*

She rolled her eyes as a silent peanut-butter commercial gave way to live coverage at the river.

She dropped her hands onto the table. Her heart leaped into her throat. She scanned the room full of oblivious people, all pecking at their phone screens or chatting with friends. Rita leaned across the table, wholly focused on the scrolling text beneath the coverage.

"Witnesses reported seeing members of the Cade County Sheriff's Department and Coroner's Office at this location early this morning. Crime scene tape and a number of road blocks have been put in place as the hours progress. Behind me you can see the continued presence of the CCSD. Our question is, why?"

The young reporter on-screen pressed her fingers against one ear and dropped her gaze. When she raised her face to the camera once more, her skin had gone ghost white.

"Sources have confirmed a body was pulled from the river just after sunrise."

Chapter Four

Rita rose on shaky legs as images of the coroner's van crossed the communal screen, a turbulent Ohio River in the background. An old factory and a dozen feline silhouettes anchored the scene.

Her ears began to ring as she strode conspicuously to the door, bumping into people and chair legs while watching the television for any last-minute announcements.

The wind was brisk and nippy as she shoved free of the coffee shop's warmth and safety onto the sidewalk where anyone could see her. Namely a nefarious deputy and the other man from the docks. The one who'd had blood on his dress shirt. She hurried to the little borrowed car and shoved her purse and laptop bag across the console. Rita locked the doors and checked her mirrors before dropping her forehead onto the steering wheel.

Think.

The men she'd seen at the docks had murdered someone. She'd heard the splash. Seen the blood.

And the men had seen her.

She raised her eyes to scan the street and sidewalks around her once more, begging her mind to focus. She couldn't stay at the coffee shop without someone noticing her imminent breakdown. She couldn't go home or back to work. The bad guys had already been there. She paused at the thought. *Bad guys.* Was this even her life?

"What do I do?" she whispered to her windshield. *They know who I am. Where I work and live.* What did they want? To kill her? Why? She hadn't seen anything. Couldn't even identify them. Though she had gotten a good look at the deputy who came to her office this morning and could give a rough description of the other guy—size, height, weight, but not much else. Her gaze traveled slowly to the bag on her passenger seat. *The pen.* What if it was evidence in a murder investigation, and she'd wadded it in tissues and stuffed it in a plastic baggie? There could be fingerprints or DNA evidence or an imperceptible thread. Forensics could find anything, and if the killers knew she had something linking them to the crime, they'd definitely want it back. So what should she do with it?

She considered tossing it out the window.

Her head spun as she pulled carefully into traffic. She should've told Deputy Garrett what had happened. Something in her gut said he had nothing to do with the man at her office or the crime scene. Deputy Garrett was trustworthy, and he would help her. There was no more doubt as to whether or not she'd been present for what she thought she'd been present for. She was a witness, albeit probably after the fact, to murder. And she was in danger.

It was time to do what she should've done all along.

She slowed at the traffic light and dug through her bag for the handsome deputy's business card. She'd call him as soon as she got to wherever she was going. Where was that?

The light turned green, and Rita lowered her foot against the gas pedal. The sun-bleached hula girl on her brother's dashboard bobbled. "Oh, no." A new and terrifying realization slid like ice into her stomach. If the bad guys knew who she was, where she worked and lived, then they also knew what she drove. And her little brother was currently driving it!

Rita applied brute force to the narrow pedal, racing through downtown, then over the bridge and across the river. She dialed Ryan repeatedly from every traffic light and stop sign.

No answer.

Her mind conjured ghastly images of her new silver truck rolled onto its top or sinking in the river, Ryan trapped inside.

"Hi, Ryan," she told his voice mail as calmly as possible. "It's me. Listen. I'm sorry, but I completely forgot I had a thing today, and you can't use my truck. I'll make it up to you as soon as I finish my thing." She cringed. Ryan would never accept her flimsy excuse without explanation, but she couldn't offer him anything more. Bringing him in on her mess would put him in danger. "Anyway, I'm on my way to your place now. I'll just trade you back real quick. Sit tight and I'll be there in ten."

She bit her lip, hating the lie. She'd promised Ryan

long ago that he could always trust anything she said, and until now, she'd held tight to that promise. Hopefully he'd forgive her when she was able to explain the gruesome truth.

Rita switched to back roads as the campus came into view. Main routes and intersections were bogged with student traffic and puttering locals. The little hatchback took corners with ease as she cut through the rear entrance to Ryan's neighborhood. Her much larger truck would've barely passed through the narrow alleyways with cars parked on both sides. If his car didn't smell like a gym bag filled with burger grease, she'd agree to trade with him more often.

Finally, the home Ryan shared with two other students came into view.

The only vehicle in the driveway was another old compact.

"No." Rita pulled up to the curb and stared. Where was he? Why wasn't he answering her calls? Again, the scary images beat a path through her mind. *Please*, she sent up a silent prayer, *don't let anything happen to my baby brother.*

Her phone buzzed against her lap and she jumped.

Ryan's name appeared on the screen beside a tiny envelope. He'd sent her a text message.

She released a happy sob and swiped the screen to life.

Taking exam. Can't talk.

He was at school. She wiped her eyes and pulled in long, thankful breaths. Everything was fine. Ryan was safe. She was safe. All she had to do now was switch the vehicles and report everything she'd seen last night to Cole Garrett.

No problem.

The drive though the campus was steeped in nostalgia. Fall was in the air. Mums were in bloom. Even the leafy green trees had begun to change into their pretty fall uniforms. Rita had made memories to last a lifetime on those same streets not too long ago.

Students filled the corners near streetlamps, watching the lights, waiting to cross. Probably headed to class or on another adventure they'd miss dearly someday too soon. College had been Rita's only taste of freedom before becoming the surrogate parent to a grieving teenage brother just two months after graduation.

The main lot for student commuters was nearly full. She circled twice before spotting her truck among a pack of even larger pickups. She pulled Ryan's car into an empty spot several spaces away and tucked his keys under the floor mat. Much as she hated to interrupt him again, especially knowing he was trying to take an exam, she sent a text to let him know his car was there and her truck was off-limits for the day.

Your car is in the lot with my truck. DO NOT take my truck. I'll be back for it. Meeting a friend.

She frowned at the little screen and sent a happier follow-up.

Good luck on your tests!

Rita pocketed the phone and kneaded her shaky hands, then fumbled Deputy Garrett's card into her grip. The sooner she unloaded the truth about what she thought she'd seen last night, and the possible murder evidence from her bag, the sooner she'd feel like herself again.

She double-checked for anyone who looked as if they might be following her, then began the trek across the giant lot toward a busier portion of campus. "Here goes nothing," she whispered, bringing the phone into view and tapping the numbers against her screen.

COLE LEFT HIS cruiser in the middle of the road beside West's and jogged around a line of news vans and local reporters. Crime scene officials tramped the soggy ground near the body recovery site, and a woman in a county coroner's office jacket picked through the area blocked off by yellow tape.

Cole had lost track of the fancy black car after leaving Rita Horn's place, but something in his gut told him the vehicle was significant. The timing of its appearance and haste of its departure were undeniably suspect, and given the break-in, Cole sensed a connection. Maybe Rita had been holding back about who could've wrecked her place, and maybe that certain someone owned a late-model black sedan. His hands curled into fists at his sides. The idea of someone intending her harm knotted his muscles and tightened his jaw.

West caught Cole's arrival and left the quarantined area with an expectant look. "Everything okay with the house? Was it a B and E or false alarm?"

"B and E," Cole grouched. He rubbed the back of his neck and rolled his shoulders, attempting and failing to dislodge the mound of frustration piling there. "It was Rita Horn's place."

West rocked back on his heels with a grin. "That so?"

"Yeah. You know her?"

West smiled. "I believe I do. That's the redhead from the courthouse?"

Cole worked his jaw, unimpressed that his older brother knew Rita existed. Not that he was in the market for a date. West already had a stunning wife, a toddler and a new baby on the way. And he wasn't the sort to have a wandering eye. Still, the conspiratorial look on his face was starting to tick Cole off.

"How well do you know her?" He had three brothers, and they were all known for their ability to get women into bed with a wink and a smile.

"Are you kidding?" West cocked a hip and crossed his arms. "Isn't she the one you used to talk about all the time?"

Cole shot his brother a droll look. "I mentioned her *once*, months ago, and I didn't know her name. I'd hardly call that 'all the time.'"

"Compared to the vast number of other women you never mention, once is a lot. Did you get her number?"

"Yeah. From Dispatch, but she didn't answer."

West barked a laugh and shook his head. "All right. If you're here, then everything must be fine there. So let's figure this one out." West led the way back to the river where the fog hovered like an apparition over the swollen waters, muting the view of a busy college town across the way.

"We know the victim's name was Roger Minsk." West pulled a notebook from his coat pocket and flipped the pages.

"Never heard of him."

"He hasn't been in town long. According to county records, he bought a big house upriver this summer. The maid called the station to report him missing three days ago. I haven't had time to follow up." He furrowed his brow. "She said he was a businessman who traveled."

Cole shook his head. "No one's blaming this on you. He's a grown man. With a maid." His nose wrinkled as the information settled in. Not a lot of folks in Shadow Point kept maids, even if they could afford it. "Who does that?"

West dropped his attention back to the notepad. "Well, this guy, for starters. She didn't have access to his calendar or contacts, so I wasn't in a hurry to worry. I knocked on his door that night and again yesterday. No answer. He was on our list of things to look into if he didn't show up by today. I was hoping he was on vacation."

"Did the maid say anything else?"

"She said she cleans for Minsk twice a week and nothing had changed since the last time she'd been there. It didn't look as if he'd slept in his bed the night before."

"So we don't know when he went missing, but we have a window."

West nodded. "The medical examiner will get us a time of death. I'd say we know the cause."

Right. The gunshot wound to the head was hard to miss. Cole turned back toward his cruiser. "I'll visit the maid, see what I can find out about the victim, then report back. Maybe I can even get her to let me into his place. Two birds."

"Yep." West agreed. "Do it. I'll be here if you need me. Don't forget to check in. We don't know who we're looking for or what this is about, and I don't like it."

Cole waved a hand overhead, making good time across the empty field, a list of questions for the maid solidifying in his mind.

"Deputy?" West called from the growing distance between them.

"Yeah?" Cole pivoted on his next step, for a look back at his brother, still standing sentinel at the river. He lifted his chin in question.

"Do me a favor and check in on Miss Horn while you're out. See if she needs anything."

"Yep."

West raised one arm in his direction. "Maybe dinner and a movie."

Cole turned away with a smile. "I'm keeping it professional," he called over one shoulder.

Not like West and his wife. They'd reunited last year after a decade apart. One minute, she was involved in a crime spree, and the next thing Cole knew, he was standing witness in a rented tuxedo as the two said their vows.

Pass. Cole wanted all those things one day, but he

had a lot of other things he wanted to do first. Find out who tossed that man in the river, for example.

He waved off a renegade reporter headed his way. "No comment." And ducked behind the wheel of his cruiser. This was what held Cole's interest. A puzzle. A mystery. Protecting the peace. These were the things that kept him up at night and got him out of bed in the morning.

He pulled slowly away from the crime scene, taking note of the smattering of faces in the gathering crowd. Had one of them seen something they weren't willing to divulge? Had they been around last night, feeding cats and playing unwitting witness to murder? If his theory was right about another person being present, he could only hope they wouldn't wash up on the riverbank like Roger Minsk.

Cole's phone buzzed against his ribs, pulling his attention away from the crowd. He freed it from his inside jacket pocket. Rita Horn's number lit the little screen. "Deputy Garrett," he answered, already pointing his car in the direction of her home. A rush of anxiety tightened his grip. If she was in trouble...

"Hi, um, this is Rita Horn. From this morning. I had the ransacked house."

An easy smile curved his lips. She was okay. His foot eased back on the gas. "I remember. How's the lock working out?"

"Okay, I think. I'm not home, actually. I hoped we could talk somewhere in person."

The background noise registered with him, then dozens of voices and...

"Is that a marching band?"

"Uh. I think. I can't see it from here, but it's football season, so I guess. I'm at the college in Rivertown. Can you meet me at the library near the square? Do you know it?"

Cole took the next left toward the bridge over the river. "Sure. Can you tell me what's going on?"

Wind crackled through the phone. Rita didn't speak.

"Go on," he urged. "You called for a reason. Let me have it."

"Okay," she began, then paused once more.

"Rita?"

"I was at the docks last night, and I think I'm being stalked by a murderer."

Chapter Five

Cole's gut fisted. His fingers whitened on the steering wheel, and he rammed his foot against the gas pedal. *Rita was the witness.* She'd fed the cats. *Of course she had.* He shook his head as the cruiser raced across Memorial Bridge. Away from West and the crime scene. Directly toward the insanely captivating redhead who fed homeless cats and people, and raised a teenage brother when she was barely done being a teen herself. Toward a woman whose kind heart and good deeds had just gotten her into serious trouble.

If she was right about being followed, Cole had to reach her before the killer did.

Cole had no idea why Mr. Minsk was killed, but whatever had tainted his life should never have crossed paths with Rita Horn. Not now. Not ever.

Definitely not on Cole's watch.

He eased his foot off the pedal as the small college town popped up around him with its spirit shops and mascot-logoed flags on every lamppost. The pounding of a marching band's bass line thundered in the distance.

Hordes of distracted students took their sweet time

jaywalking across the street in front of him, holding him up, keeping him from Rita. He tapped his thumbs against the wheel and considered using the siren, though it had no jurisdiction here. The water behind them had officially yielded his badge void. "Come on," he growled, the fear in Rita's voice still ringing in his ears.

The street cleared, and the light overhead turned red. "Dammit!"

Cole snatched his phone off the passenger seat where he'd tossed it and dialed West. He should've called him sooner. Told him about Rita's confession. Asked where the library was. Now he was wasting precious time and growing unhappier by the second.

"Sheriff Garrett." West answered on the first ring.

Cole rolled his eyes. "Hey. I'm over in Rivertown, meeting Rita. She called to tell me she was at the docks last night."

The line was silent for a long beat before West cursed quietly under his breath. "She bought the cat food."

"Looks like it. At least now we know why someone tossed her place this morning." And why she'd been so on edge. It also explained why she'd left work feeling sick, but hadn't looked it. "She thinks the killer's stalking her."

West swore again. Louder this time. "Why are you in Rivertown? Bring her to the station so we can talk."

The light changed, and Cole inched into the intersection before another swarm of students could hold him up again. "I'm not clear on the *why* yet. She asked me to meet her at the library. I think her little brother is a student here. She could be checking up on him."

"Was he with her last night?" West asked. "Did she tell you anything else?"

"No." Cole scanned the crowded sidewalks. "Where is the library?" He could find it himself with a little more time. The campus wasn't big, but time was something Cole didn't have to spare. "I haven't been here since high school. Were there always this many people?" He checked each passing face for the woman he longed to save, but she wasn't among the crowds.

West gave him blow-by-blow directions to the center of campus.

A white marble fountain stood proudly outside the building marked Library, spraying crystal clear water into the cloudless blue sky. Cole took the last available parking spot and fed the meter a handful of quarters before jogging through the library's front door.

RITA ORDERED A cup of hot tea and took a seat at the window inside a nearby café. The library had been uncomfortably silent and borderline terrifying. Not enough witnesses. She hadn't been able to stay. Her imagination had wreaked havoc within seconds, and she'd darted back onto the crowded, familiar streets for a deep breath of air. A café with large window and view of the library seemed a smart compromise. From here, she'd see Cole's arrival.

Rita pointed her chair at the window. Paranoia crawled over her skin like a thousand baby spiders. She couldn't shake the feeling that she wasn't safe, not even in another town. As if the bridge and river weren't enough distance to protect her from whatever was happening. She inhaled the aroma of her drink and willed the sweet steam to ease her jangled nerves. She also tried closing her lids and counting to ten.

Nothing helped.

Rita let her gaze make quick and continuous loops around the square between sips, checking the street and sidewalks in both directions. So far, no sign of Cole Garrett or any other Cade County deputies.

Good, evil or otherwise.

A clutch of women in blue-and-white hoodies crossed the street, leaving a black sedan in clear view. The vehicle crept along the street outside, dark tinted windows staring back at her, and disappeared around the corner.

Rita worked to swallow the mouthful of suddenly tasteless tea before she choked on it. *Sedans are common*, she told herself.

Breathe. Relax. Deputy Garrett is on his way.

Wasn't he? Her gaze jumped to the library entrance across the street. Where was he?

She pushed the teacup aside and leaned over the table on her elbows, stretching for a look in the direction the sedan had gone.

The little bell over the café's front door jingled, setting her back on her seat. A man strode inside. Too old to be a student. Too casual for a professor. He locked gazes with her, and Rita tilted her head to take him in. There was something in his stride that sent her heart into a fresh sprint. He lifted his brows, and Rita spun in her chair, fixing her eyes on the library outside once more.

It's not him. It's not him, she chanted mentally.

Rita kept the silent refrain going, but couldn't bring herself to believe the words. How could she be sure? She hadn't seen either man's face clearly last night, but the sedan had just rolled by... Rita peeked over her shoulder at the man, now poised at the counter.

The long angles of his arms and lean cut of his waist drew itchy memories over her skin. Was this the same man from her office earlier today? If so, what had happened to the deputy jacket?

The memory of hushed footfalls echoed in her mind, making her breaths shudder.

Her tummy rocked, and an uncomfortable sheen of sweat broke over her goose-pimpled skin. She wasn't built for this kind of life. She'd made herself sick many times with worry, always about her brother's well-being or the health and safety of others. She worried about homeless and injured animals, her fledgling garden and whether or not she'd left the iron on. Those were problems she could deal with. This...

She imagined the man at the counter in a bulky deputy's jacket, marching her way, chasing her through the night. What if he approached her discreetly and pressed a gun to her back? Then tossed her in the trunk and drove her to the river?

Nope.

She gathered the straps of her bags with hasty fingers and slid, nearly fell, off her chair, but the packed-up laptop case caught on the table's edge. "Sorry," she apologized to no one in particular, before stumbling over the table leg and ramming her shoulder into the café door on her way out. Cole or no Cole, Rita couldn't stay. She ducked her head against the number of stunned faces still inside the café, now watching her as she passed the window outside.

The newcomer's eyes were narrow, and his lips were turned down. He made a move for the door, but Rita didn't wait to see where he was headed.

Her flying heart carried her through knots and clusters of students on street corners and outside shops. She darted around a lamppost and into a bookstore she knew had a back exit that opened into a brick courtyard with a gate to an alley. She'd used them both many times during her four-year tenure in Rivertown, perpetually running late to class, often the result of a novel she couldn't put down.

Street noise filled her ears as she landed in the store's rear courtyard. A sprinkle of quiet students in wooden lounge chairs glanced her way, then back to their phones or books, unconcerned by her sudden and probably wild appearance.

Rita followed the picket fence at a crouch. She peeked over the top once, after a strong internal pep talk to convince herself it was important to see the bad guy before he saw her.

She stopped at the rear gate and pressed her forehead to the cool wooden slats. Anxiety twisted her gut and paralyzed her limbs. Maybe she didn't have to go out there again. Maybe Cole could meet here where she was.

She rubbed her sweat-slicked palms over her jeans,

one by one, juggling the phone with each move. Then she hunched her shoulders over her cell phone and sent a text to Deputy Garrett.

Where are you?

Cole's response was immediate. I'm at the library. Where are you?

Of course. He'd gone straight to their meeting place, like she should have. The silence and lack of bodies hadn't frightened him the way it had her.

Rita pulled in a restorative breath and let it out with resolve. Everything was okay now. The library was just down the alley and across the street. She only needed to leave the safety of the fence and get on with it.

She nodded at her screen, then typed On my way.

The phone rang in her shaky hand as she shoved the creaky gate open, creating an escape hatch from the enclosed bookshop patio. Cole's number appeared on her screen.

Her heart settled at the sight of it. "Hi."

"Hey." Cole's voice was strong and steady. "I'm standing outside the library. Tell me where you are, and I'll come to you. You don't have to walk alone."

"I appreciate that. I might be wrong, but I think one of the men I saw last night is here, too."

"Where?"

"Possibly in the café across from the library. I got nervous and left. Now I'm leaving the bookshop on River Drive. I cut through when I thought I was being followed." And if she made it to Cole fast enough, she might make it home without a nervous breakdown.

Rita rolled her shoulders back, borrowing from his confidence.

She stepped into the midday sun and examined the passing faces. "I don't see him now. It was probably nothing. I might be losing my mind, actually."

"You're not." Cole assured her. "You've been through a trauma. Give yourself some credit for brilliance."

"Brilliance?"

"You called me for help."

Rita snickered. "An ego to go with the face. Isn't that always the way?"

"You like my face?"

She smiled against the receiver, enjoying the sudden and blatant curiosity in Cole's voice. He had to know he was handsome. According to the rumors, not that she listened, there were four Garrett brothers, all gorgeous, all lawmen, and all terminally single until recently. But that was fine. She didn't need a date. She needed a protector, and the rumors about the Garretts being unstoppable forces of nature were repeated with as much fervor as those about their sexual prowess.

Those were the rumors she'd put her hope in.

She hurried away from the courtyard. Through a wall of ambling jocks and across the little street. The weight of her situation rolled away as the school's library sign came into view. The door was only ten yards away, just around the next corner. Safety was so close she could throw a stone and hit it. "I see the fountain," she said. "I'm almost…"

The sound of a revving engine cut through her words. A black sedan moved down the street in her direction.

Her mouth opened as the car bore down on her, but only a strangled sound emerged.

"Rita?" Cole barked through the receiver.

Her limbs were leaden as the car tore through the alley in her direction, increasing in speed and chasing students out of its way with a growl.

Her heart ached through to her backbone.

"Rita!" Cole hollered. "Move!" His voice echoed through the phone's speaker and in the air. Cole appeared in the distance, running full speed from the café where she'd seen the creepy man. "Run!"

Adrenaline shot through her limbs like lightning bolts, propelling her suddenly away from the car, around café tables on the sidewalk outside a pizza shop and down the narrow street once filled with students. She pumped her arms and legs as the engine roared closer and lunged for the historic marble fountain moments later, tossing her phone and bags before colliding smartly with the fountain's edge and soaring headlong into the recycled water. Her shins and palms were on fire from the collision before her head cracked against the carved angel's feet.

Her face submerged and, for a moment, there was nothing but icy water everywhere.

She arose with a gasp, pulling in lungfuls of oxygen and scrambling around the fountain's center.

The sound of squealing brakes and screaming people snapped her thoughts back into focus. The car!

"Stop!" Cole's demand rang through the chaos, much closer now.

She wiped her eyes and spun in search of the voice she'd only known a short while, but could somehow pick out of a wailing crowd.

The engine revved once more as the car changed direction and roared softly into the distance.

She collapsed backward into the water, fighting an onslaught of tears. Her limbs trembled and her teeth chattered. She sat upright, knees pulled to her chest, overcome with panic and confusion.

Dozens of people stared openly, pointing their cell phones in her direction. Her brother was going to die of humiliation when he saw the footage and be infinitely angry she hadn't opened up to him about what happened at the docks.

She dropped her head forward and begged her mind to think.

How could she possibly explain this away?

A set of strong hands wrapped around her elbows and hoisted her from the water with a whoosh.

Rita screamed. Her feet found purchase on the ground outside the fountain, and she locked her palms together on instinct to thrust against her assailant's chest, sending him back several steps.

Cole relented, palms up as he widened his stance and waited. "Hey. It's just me." He watched silently as her scrambled brain put the pieces together.

"Cole!" Recognition hit, and Rita flung herself at him. She buried her face against his shoulder and exhaled the suffocating terror from her lungs. "I thought

I was dead. I thought he'd kill me right here in front of everyone."

Cole's broad, warm hands found the small of her back and pressed her to him. "You're okay, Rita." His heart thrummed beneath her ear, chest rising and falling in quick bursts.

The sound of her name on his lips sent a shiver down her spine. The soft scents of spearmint, earth and aftershave that wafted off his heated skin didn't help.

She peeled herself away with burning cheeks. "You're soaked." She brushed the sodden fabric of his uniform shirt with shaky hands. "I'm soaked and now… I'm so sorry."

Rita locked her knees in frustration, and the tears began to flow.

"Hey." Cole pulled her back against him and stroked her sopping hair. "I won't let anyone hurt you. Okay? But you've got to trust me." He took her hands in his, and led her away from the wretched fountain and massive crowd. "First, let's get you out of here. I need to call this in, and you need something dry to wear. I've got towels and a first aid kit in the gym bag in my cruiser. How hurt are you?"

"I'm not."

He turned her palm up in his, both their hands now painted with her blood. "No?"

"Scrapes. From the marble."

He nodded stiffly. "What else?"

Her legs were sore and her head was fuzzy. "Bruises. Ow." Her vision blurred. "I think I hit my…" Rita's knees buckled and the world went black.

Chapter Six

Cole stroked wet hair from Rita's face as he buckled her into the passenger seat of his car. This day had gone from strange to downright bizarre in a matter of hours. Luckily, Rita would be okay. "Hey."

Her eyes flitted open then pulled shut.

"Rita?" Cole pressed a palm to her cheek. "You with me?"

She squirmed, apparently confused by the seat belt. Her eyes widened and her arms swung for him.

Cole dodged the blow. That wouldn't happen again. He collected her wrists in one of his hands and put on his warmest smile. "You shouldn't hit lawmen. There's a law against that. Plus, it hurts." He made a show of rubbing his chest where she'd landed the earlier hit.

Color rushed to her cheeks. "Sorry." She squirmed to take in her new surroundings. "What happened?"

"You passed out. I carried you to my car." Cole tugged her safety belt, making sure it was securely latched. "How's your head?"

She groaned.

Cole flashed a penlight in her direction. "Can you follow the light?"

She squinted, but got the job done.

"Okay." He lifted a finger before shutting her inside the cruiser and rounding the hood to the driver's side. Behind the wheel, he twisted for a look in her direction. "You were chased by a lunatic in a black sedan. Tinted windows. No plates. Any chance you got a look at the driver?"

She shook her head.

"You would've been killed if you hadn't dived into the fountain. You hit your head doing that. Then you hit me. Then you passed out. And here we are."

She rubbed her eyes and groaned.

Cole pointed his cruiser toward the bridge, waving to a set of campus security officers. "Those guys showed up as I was hauling you off the street. I barely caught you before you hit your head again." He chuckled. "You were right in the middle of telling me how well you felt."

"I think I have a concussion."

"You don't." He smiled, happy to know that was true. She was fine. Slightly banged up, but all things considered, Rita was stellar. "It wasn't the head injury that knocked you out, but that goose egg is going to look a lot worse before it starts looking better."

Rita dissolved against his passenger seat. Her fingers sought the wound. She winced when she found it.

"Shock will do that to people. The fainting, not the goose egg. Anyway, you're fine now."

"Except someone still wants to kill me."

"Yeah." There was that. He ground his teeth. He needed to fix that. "You're having a bad day."

She laughed humorlessly, eyes fixed on the world outside her window. "Very bad."

"And you're all wet."

"I need to go home," she said.

"Already on it." Cole took the bridge back to Shadow Point at half the speed he'd used to arrive in Rivertown.

Rita closed her eyes. "Why are you so calm, and how do you know I'm okay?" Her teeth chattered.

Cole ached to stroke the curve of her clenched jaw. "You're with me now. You're definitely going to make it, Horn."

She rolled her head in his direction, blinking through tear-filled eyes. "And how can you be sure I'm not concussed?"

"Medical school."

Rita's rosebud mouth pulled into a droll expression. "Of course."

"I dropped out," he said, "so I'm not a doctor, but I was a medic in the army, and I've been bandaging up my brothers all my life. My uncle's an EMT, too, so that helped."

Rita straightened in her seat. "Wait a minute. You quit medical school to be a deputy?"

"Law's in the blood, I guess."

"I guess," she agreed. "Clearly also a hero complex."

"Not the first time I've been accused of that. I guess we have something in common."

Rita wrinkled her nose. "What?"

"The hero complex." He watched for understanding

that never came, then tried again. "What do you call what you do?"

"Paperwork?"

"No," he corrected. "Feeding stray cats and making lunches for the homeless. You know all their names, and I don't even know all the bailiffs. What do you call yourself, if not a hero?"

A wave of pink spread over her cheeks. "Nothing. I'm just...trying."

Cole worked to redirect his thoughts from that blush and all the other ways he'd like to summon it.

A few creative images came immediately to mind.

Rita's lips parted. She dropped her sweet hazel gaze to her lap before raising her eyes to him once more. "I try to make a difference."

Her words hit Cole in the chest. So much kindness in one small package. How did a woman like Rita Horn go unattached? If Cole were looking for something serious, which he wasn't, and she wasn't an endangered civilian in his care, which she was, maybe there could have been something between them.

Like what? He chastised himself. *Pull it together, Garrett.*

Ten silent minutes later, Cole pulled into Rita's driveway.

Rita unlocked the door and welcomed him inside.

The house was exactly as he remembered. No one had been back while Rita was out. Then again, he'd already known the person responsible for overturning her place was likely the same one driving the sedan across the river.

He helped himself to a seat on her couch while she went to change clothes.

Cole checked his texts and listened to the handful of messages that had collected during his drive back to town. Campus security had conveyed the details of the attack to their local authorities. Rivertown police were interviewing the mass of witnesses and would report to West on the matter.

The phone vibrated in his hand, and West's face appeared on his screen.

"You got something?" Cole moved the phone to his ear.

"Yeah, a pair of empty seats across from my desk. Where are you?"

"Rita's place. She's cleaning up from her fall in the fountain."

"Get her here as soon as you can. Meanwhile, tell me what you learned." The sound of West's creaky desk chair echoed in the quiet background. Cole could practically see his older brother rubbing the stress lines off his forehead.

"Nothing," he admitted, "but we'll head over to the sheriff's department next."

"No!" Rita appeared on the stairs, white as a ghost and looking fit to run. She'd showered and changed at an impressive speed, and from the looks of her, she didn't plan to stay put.

"Why not?" Cole's voice sounded in time with West's through the line.

"Did she say no?" West barked. "Why the hell not?"

Cole studied the fresh fear in Rita's eyes. "I'll call

you back." He tossed the phone onto the coffee table and scooted to the edge of the couch, hands clasped between his knees.

Rita took the final few stairs slowly, an apology written on her face. "I'm sorry. I know that's not what you wanted to hear, and you've already done so much."

"Why don't you have a seat," Cole suggested. "Tell me why you look half terrified to go to the sheriff's department. What will happen there?"

"I don't know." She wet her lips and lowered onto the cushion beside him, leaving only a few inches from his knee to hers. "I need to tell you something, but you aren't going to like it."

"Try me." He relaxed his position, trading the forward lean for a casual slouch and pivot in her direction.

She drew her feet beneath her and pulled in a long breath. Her scent drifted to him in a cloud of temptation.

"Rita?" he pushed. "It's okay. You can tell me anything."

Her emotion-filled eyes enticed him to reach for her. She scanned the room before setting her gaze remorsefully on Cole. "The man I saw at the docks last night was a Cade County deputy."

RITA WATCHED AS Cole's expression stretched from shock to disbelief.

"No." He shook his head. "No way."

She released a deep sigh. "Yes. I saw him."

"Who?"

"I didn't get his name, if that's what you're asking, but one of you has been following me all day. To my work. To my brother's school. You'll have to excuse me if I'm in no hurry to deliver myself to him at the station."

"Whoa." Cole raised his palms. "Let's start again. How do you know he's a Cade County deputy?"

"I saw him. The man at the docks, the same one who visited my office, wore a jacket just like yours. Actually, it's possible they were two different men," she corrected. "Either way, I saw the Cade County Sheriff's Department logo on the jacket both times. I'm sure of it."

"What about the man you saw in Rivertown?"

"No jacket." Intuition had told her the man from the café was dangerous, but she couldn't be sure he was the same man from the docks. "And I didn't see him driving the car."

Cole nodded. "That's okay. You remember what he looks like?"

"Yes."

"That's a good start." Cole handed his phone to her. "I believe you saw a man in a deputy's jacket, but it had to be a fake. Folks see a lawman, they tend to look the other way."

Rita bit her lip. Personally, she found the uniform captivating, but she wasn't about to say so.

"There are only six of us," Cole continued. "West, me and four other men I love like family." He pointed to the phone screen. Pictures from a picnic centered the frame. "Move through those. See if your man's in there. The whole team made an appearance that day, and I've got pictures of everyone."

Rita studied each photo, taking in the details, peeking into a day in Cole's life. She had to admit it looked like fun. Volleyball. Horseshoes. Enough food to feed an army and enough people to form one. "This is all your family?"

"Most of it. Not everyone could make it, but quite a few friends showed up, too. Like the other deputies. Everyone stopped in before and after their shifts."

"Reunion?" she guessed.

"Nah. Housewarming for one of my brothers and his new wife." Cole crossed his arms and smiled. "It was a good day."

Rita shook her head in awe. "We've never had that. The military moved our family too often to really grow roots. People were usually nice, but it was always just Mom, Ryan and me. Now it's just the two of us, and Ryan's got his own life across the river."

"Sounds lonely."

"It can be," she admitted. "So I reach out to others."

Cole drifted closer. Conflict burned in his deep blue eyes.

Rita turned her attention back to his phone. She looked at each face carefully. "I didn't get a good look at the man's face last night, but my gut says he's not here. He's shorter and more heavily muscled than these men, built more like the man from the café." She returned the phone to him, then stood and moved onto the stairs. "I have something I want to give you."

His cheek ticked up. He hooked one boot over the opposite knee and opened his arms along the back of the couch. Whatever he was thinking, he kept it to himself.

Her tiger cat sashayed in his direction, blinking curious green eyes.

"Be right back." Rita grabbed her purse off her bed and returned to his side. "I found this on the docks beside a big puddle of blood." Her tongue stuck to the roof of her mouth, preventing her from saying anything more. Instead, she liberated the pen from her bag and handed it to Cole.

Cole traded her the mewing tiger cat on his lap for the evidence in her hand. "This was with the blood?"

"Yeah. I put it in the baggie so it wouldn't get ruined. I think that was what they were after when they broke in here today." She stroked the kitty's head and nuzzled him close to her cheek. "At first I thought one of the cats was hurt. That's why I ignored the no-trespassing sign."

Cole chuckled. He rolled smart blue eyes up at her and smiled. "This pen could be all we need to find the killer. You did good, Horn."

"Thanks." She hid her face in the feline's fur.

Cole watched.

Her puffy white Persian, Snowball, appeared at Cole's feet. She eyeballed the tiger cat in Rita's arms, then turned to the deputy on her couch. Snowball climbed onto Cole's lap and flopped onto her side.

Cole's hands dived into her soft, downy fur and drew out a long enthusiastic purr. "How many cats do you have?"

"Three." She cleared her throat. "I've had more, but these guys get territorial. When I have more than three, it's because I'm fostering until someone else can find a forever home."

Cole's smile waned.

"What?"

"No. Nothing." He set the cat aside and took a spin around the room. He rubbed the top of his head. "Someone knows you have that pen."

"I think so. Yeah."

He turned to face her. "Then we should probably get going."

"Where?"

"Look." He moved cautiously in her direction. "I know you don't want to visit the sheriff's department, but West has questions of his own for you."

Rita stepped back.

Cole flashed an easy, heart-melting smile, and he extended an upturned palm. "I can keep you safe. Do you trust me?"

Rita considered her answer. She trusted Cole. Maybe West. She hadn't recognized any of the other men in the photos. Maybe Cole was right. Maybe the jacket had been a fake. "Fine." Rita collected her purse and laptop bag, dragging both high onto her shoulder. "I can't believe my laptop didn't wind up in the fountain."

Cole dropped his hand, but held the smile. "It was on the cement, right about where you dived in. You're lucky it isn't a pile of plastic bits and keys."

Rita ripped into the bag for a look at her device. Everything seemed intact. "Thank goodness." She smiled in relief. "Wait." A new worry presented itself in Rita's mind. "How do you suppose that black car was able to find me in another town?"

Cole pushed his hands into his pockets. "I saw one like it outside your house when I left today. I tried following, but I lost it in traffic. It could've been following you all morning. Or..." He turned in a sudden circle, lips parted and eyes narrowed. "Someone trashed your house but didn't take anything."

"I had the pen with me. In my bag."

Cole raised his hand once more. "Can I see your bag?"

"Sure." She unhooked both sets of straps from her shoulder and handed them over.

"Did you have both these bags with you all day? Even at work?"

"Not the laptop. I use my work computer while I'm there."

Cole turned the bag inside out, sweeping his hand over the material in a methodical pattern. His eyebrows rose, and his hand withdrew from the bag with a tiny black dot on the end of one finger. "Is this yours?"

"What is it?"

Cole tipped his hand between them, examining the little plastic thing on his finger. "Someone put a tracker in your laptop bag."

Rita covered her mouth. Who would do something like that? Who could do something like that? Not an average thug. The other man's suit and bloody dress shirt came back to mind. "There was a second man," she said, realizing only then that she'd never told Cole about him. "He was dressed up. A suit and tie, but his face was in shadows."

Cole stretched impossibly taller. "I don't know what you stumbled into, but I think it's time I get you out of here." He grabbed his phone and swiped the screen to life. "Pack a bag and let's go."

Chapter Seven

Rita admired the view as Cole parked the cruiser in front of a sensible Craftsman-style bungalow near the national forest. Forgotten barns peppered the rolling landscape, leaned precariously against the horizon. Overgrown fields swayed and stretched in the afternoon breeze, contained loosely by a sturdy-looking pasture fence. They'd negotiated a trade on the way over. She'd agreed to stay with Cole temporarily, just until the killer was caught or a more secure option arose, and he'd agreed to get West to question her at his place instead of the station.

Rita gave her handsome driver an appraising look. "This is where you live?"

"Yeah." He cracked the door and stepped onto the gravel.

Rita watched in the rearview mirror as he popped the trunk and shouldered her bags, arriving a moment later at her door. "You realize you have to get out of the car to get inside the house, right?" he asked through her still-closed door.

Rita joined him on the long narrow drive, taking in

the distance to the road and nearest homes, mere dots on the horizon. "This is really secluded."

"Private," he corrected. "It takes my family longer to get here than anywhere else, so they're more likely to knock on West's or Blake's door than mine." He cocked an eyebrow. "I had a place in town for a few years, but I could barely think between doorbell rings."

Rita considered the new information. "I didn't peg you for a loner." More like Mr. Congeniality.

"I'm not," he said, opening the front door. "I love my family. My friends."

"But you like to be alone," she finished.

Cole turned a curious look in her direction. "Yeah."

Rita nodded. "Me, too."

Cole lifted a finger as they crossed the threshold. "Wait here."

Rita watched from her position in the open living area as Cole made a sweep of the home before returning to her side. From where she stood, it was easy to see the kitchen, back door and loft, and a hallway to another set of rooms.

He raised his easy smile. "Ready for the tour?"

Rita hesitated. It had been a long time since a man had invited her to his home. "Sure." Reluctantly she followed him through the modest rooms, mostly decorated in outdoor equipment and pictures of him and his friends doing everything from fishing to hiking. She imagined clinging to his middle as she joined him on one of the mud-soaked four-wheelers or drenched with lake water after a dive off his boat.

Clearly, the stress was taking a toll on her mind.

Cole dropped her bags on the end of a tidy bed in an otherwise messy room. His style was clearly bachelor minimalist, but this room looked like one where he was always in a hurry. Clothes were draped over the hamper and a corner chair. Stacks of jeans lined the wall behind an open closet door.

"Sorry." Cole tossed stray items into the closet and kicked the door shut. "This room doesn't get a lot of attention. I'm always on my way in or out, so…"

She turned her eyes away from the bed. Either local rumors about his nightlife were exaggerated, or Cole just didn't bring the parade of women here. Either way, she stupidly liked the idea that he'd invited her. "It's fine. Where will you sleep?"

"Won't." The word was out in an instant, and Cole headed back into the hall.

"Why not?"

"Well, for one thing, I don't sleep well. Not since the military. For another—" he turned to look at her over his shoulder "—as long as you're with me, I'm on duty."

"Oh." She caught up with him in the narrow hall. "I can stay at a hotel. You shouldn't lose sleep over me."

He gave a disbelieving laugh, as if she'd hit on some inside joke. "I'll survive."

Cole stripped his uniform shirt off, exposing a plain white T-shirt beneath. He hung the button-down on the back of a chair pulled up to the kitchen island, then went to open the refrigerator. "Let's eat, and then we can figure out what's next."

"You don't know?" Rita climbed onto a seat at the

counter and fought a new round of panic bubbling in her core.

"Not yet," he said, no trace of concern in his tone. Cole collected glasses from the cabinet and dropped stacks of ice into them. "It's early and you still have a lot to tell me. Plus, I need to talk with West. He's been on the case since before dawn." A body in the river, a break-in at Rita's, an attempted hit-and-run in Rivertown all before two o'clock. If the pace kept up, it was going to be one hell of a night.

"How LONG DO you think I'll be here?" she asked. "Until morning? Longer? What will people think? How long will Mrs. Wilcox have to watch my cats? Can I go to work tomorrow or should I call off?"

Cole set a glass in front of her. "Drink this."

"What is it?"

"Ice water." He looked her over carefully. "How are you feeling? Besides afraid?"

She forced her attention away from his lips, ignored the way his T-shirt fit his lean body as if it had been cut just for him, and searched for an answer that had nothing to do with the butterflies in her knotted tummy. "I'm not thinking clearly." That was true enough. She gulped the water. "Probably stress and the head injury."

Cole rounded the counter with concern in his eyes. "What do you mean?" He turned the seat of her stool until she faced him, then crouched to meet her at eye level. "Your thoughts are unclear? How's your vision?"

"Fine. I thought you said I was okay."

"That was before you said you aren't thinking clearly.

What if I missed something?" He raised steady palms to outline her face, then brushed away the swath of bangs she'd arranged over the bump on her forehead.

Rita shivered.

"My hands are probably cold," he warned, flicking his gaze to the glass of ice water he'd delivered to her.

"They're nice," she said.

He pulled a penlight from his pocket with a smile and pointed it at her. "Follow this."

She trailed the pen with her eyes. "I didn't mean I couldn't think. Just that I'm thinking crazy thoughts."

Cole lifted a questioning brow, but put the light away. "One more thing, if you don't mind." He leaned closer, running his palms over her neck and shoulders, enveloping her in the deliciously masculine scent of him. "Any unusual pains? Anything that doesn't seem right to you?"

"No." Everything seemed right to her.

"Neck pain beyond the bruises?"

"No."

"Double vision? Seeing spots? Nausea?" His caring eyes drifted back to her face.

Rita's heart pounded maniacally in her chest. Surely he could hear that. *Could he hear that?* She shot her panicked gaze up to meet his.

Cole narrowed his eyes. "Do I make you nervous?"

"Absolutely." Though not in the way he'd meant. Rita had no doubt Cole could protect her from outside threats. It was her reckless heart that worried her. She knew already, maybe had known even before they officially met, that she could easily lose herself to a man like this. They were too rare, the catch every woman dreamed of finding but no one got to keep.

He cocked his head, zeroing in. "Why, exactly?"

She pressed her eyes shut, forcing herself to remember that Cole was only doing his job, and that what she wanted in a companion was so much more than he would ever give. A court clerk had caught her watching him once, and the woman had been quick to let her know she'd graduated with Cole Garrett, and he hadn't even taken a date to prom because he wanted to keep his options open.

If he couldn't commit to one woman for a single prom, Rita's heart was surely doomed.

Then again, maybe a night in his arms would be worth the penance.

"Rita?"

"Hmm?"

"Sandwiches? Soup?" Cole made a pained face. "I have no idea what you eat."

"What?" Her mind scrambled to catch up. "Food?" Shame burned in her cheeks. He was trying to feed her. To be a gentleman. And she'd been contemplating the value of her virtue.

Cole watched intently. "Are you sure you're okay? You're flushed again. Do you want to lay down?"

"No," she nearly screamed. No beds. "I like sandwiches."

He relented his too-close position with a shake of his head. "All right." Cole returned to the business side of the island and opened his refrigerator.

Rita pulled her wits back together. "I'm sorry I didn't

want to go to the sheriff's department. I know I'm putting your brother out by dragging him here instead." She focused on the extraordinary view through Cole's bay window. An array of autumn-touched trees swayed in the distance. "I'm being ridiculous. I should've just gone."

"It's fine," he said with a grin. "Very little puts West out. He's accommodating to a fault."

A cruiser rolled into view on Cole's long gravel drive, and Rita's heart stopped. "Cole."

"What?" He manifested at her side, then marched to the window for a look outside. "Oh. Here he is now."

"How can you know for sure that it's him? What if it's not him?"

"The cars are numbered and his says Sheriff."

Rita worked the information through her mind. "What if someone hurt him and took his cruiser?"

Cole barked a laugh. "Never gonna happen, but that's a funny thought."

She shot him a crazy face. "You guys aren't invincible, you know."

The doorbell stopped Cole from responding. "Hold that thought." He opened the door for the sheriff, a man she also recognized from the courthouse. Equally handsome. Slightly older. Significantly more uptight.

Rita's phone buzzed in her pocket with a text from Ryan. His exams were over, and he still wanted to use her truck.

She responded swiftly, insisting she was on her way to get the pickup now, and Ryan should leave it in the lot. She hit Send, then grimaced internally over yet another lie.

After a brief round of whispering in acronyms, the Garretts approached her shoulder to shoulder, a six-foot wall of testosterone and unwavering confidence.

Rita leaned back in her chair, adding an inch of distance.

West pressed his hat to his torso with one broad hand. "Miss Horn. I'm Cade County Sheriff West Garrett."

Cole rolled his eyes and crossed his arms. "Call him West."

"Please," West concurred. "If you don't mind, I have a few questions about what happened to you today and what went on at the docks last night."

Rita looked at Cole.

"Have a seat," Cole instructed his brother. "I'm making us a little something to eat."

COLE SET OUT an assembly line for sandwiches. He'd wanted to impress Rita with something better than a middle-school lunch, but he couldn't think straight after the way she'd looked at him when he asked if he made her nervous. He'd wanted her to know that she could trust him. That none of the Cade County deputies would hurt her, and whoever she'd seen in that jacket had been a fake.

But that look.

Her cheeks had flushed and her gaze had drifted to his mouth and lingered. The dark, heated expression on her sweet face had done things to him he didn't like. Not with her. The images clogging his mind weren't meant for someone like Rita Horn. She was a good girl, and women like her weren't supposed to look at him like that. They were supposed to want stockbrokers in suits with big-money careers and 401Ks.

Thankfully, West had arrived to put his mind back into work mode.

West took the seat beside Rita. "Did you see a cruiser last night?"

"No. Just the sedan and two men."

"Today?"

"No." She looked to Cole again. A habit she was beginning to develop. One he liked more than he should.

Cole plated the sandwiches and delivered them to the counter. "Cruisers have GPS. West can pull up the history. See if one was near the river last night or your house today."

West nodded. "Already done. None of ours were. I'm trying to figure what else the man with the deputy jacket has in his costume trunk. Good to know he doesn't have a cruiser. I can't have a lunatic pulling folks over." He cast Cole a deflated look. "The width of the track marks near the docks line up with a standard sedan, but that's as much as we can tell about the car that made them."

"I figured." Cole rubbed his hands on a towel.

West took a bite of his sandwich and focused on Rita. "What else can you tell me?"

"I knew the victim," Rita said. She shielded her mouth with one small hand while she chewed. "I saw his picture on the news."

"What do you mean, you knew him?" Cole asked.

West shot him an amused look.

Rita finished chewing before she answered. "He'd visited the municipal building a lot lately. I saw him there several times in the last week or two. I assumed he was a lawyer."

"Real estate developer," West corrected. "Do you know who he was seeing in the building?"

"No." Rita shrugged. "I never spoke to him. He was just hard to miss, so I noticed."

Cole cocked a hip.

West smiled against the edge of his sandwich. "Hard to miss?"

"Sure." Rita looked from brother to brother. "Most folks around here are low-key. Laid-back. They move slower. Talk softer. Smile more." She pursed her lips. "This guy was different. Always in a rush. Back poker straight. Flat expression. Thousand-dollar suit. He was just…off."

West made a note in his pocket-size notebook. "Cole mentioned a person of concern in the café today. Someone who made you nervous. What did that guy look like?"

Cole pressed his palms against the counter. "If we can find him in the criminal database we'll get a name."

West pointed at his brother. "We can use that to see how he's connected to the victim." He turned back to Rita. "Would you know him if you saw him again?"

"Yes."

"I'll log on to the database with her," Cole said. "No problem."

"Good." West finished his sandwich and dusted his hands together. "I'll head down to the municipal building when they open tomorrow morning and pull the surveillance tapes. See if I can find Minsk and figure out where he was going."

Cole nodded. "I'm still going to give the victim's maid a call." He tipped his head toward Rita. "I got off track earlier."

West smiled. "Let me know how it goes."

Cole stared. He could feel Rita's eyes on him. "Yep."

"Well, all right." West headed for the door. "Thanks for the sandwich. Text me if you think of anything else. Otherwise, let's hit this again tomorrow. Thank you for your time, Miss Horn."

"Of course," she said.

West hesitated. He fixed his gaze on Rita and leaned in conspiratorially. "You've had a rough day, but if anyone can keep you safe, it's this guy." He winked at Cole.

Cole made a face. "Goodbye."

West stuffed the brown sheriff's hat back on his head. "I'm going to see if I can make a dent in the paperwork before the next disaster strikes. This has been some kind of day."

Cole agreed. He locked the front door behind him.

"West seemed nice," Rita said, heading back to the kitchen. She delivered empty plates and cups to the sink.

"You don't have to do that." Cole squeezed into the space at her side and turned off the water. "Don't wash my dishes."

She flicked her wet fingertips at him. "You cooked. I clean up."

"No."

Rita turned on him, petal-pink nails latched over the sexy curves of her hips. "Are you always so bossy?"

"Yes." He rubbed his forehead, hating the irrational feeling of attachment coursing through him. Rita Horn was practically a stranger. Beautiful, kindhearted and sexy as hell, but a stranger.

Cole relaxed against the counter. "I can pull up the database after I call the victim's maid. Come on." He motioned for her to follow him to the living room. "Leave the dishes. Make yourself comfortable."

"Fine." Rita curled onto the couch and pulled a pillow over her lap.

Cole punched the television on and went for his phone.

His favorite movie was playing when he returned. "Sorry. That must've still been in the queue."

"Wait." She waved a hand at him. "I love this one."

Cole fell onto the cushion beside her. "You're kidding."

"No. This is great."

He stretched an arm over the back of the couch and worked the screen of his cell phone with his opposite thumb. "I think we're going to be friends."

"Agreed."

Cole dared a look in her direction, ignoring the tightening of his gut. "Am I still making you nervous?"

"Yeah." Rita leaned against his side with a soft sigh.

A low groan wound its way through his chest. "Back at ya."

Chapter Eight

Cole spent the night on his laptop in the living room after Rita had reluctantly agreed to get some rest in his bed. The second half of their day had been significantly quieter than the first, but twice as demanding of his professional composure. Thoughts of Rita in his room had been tough to keep at bay, but luckily the victim, Roger Minsk, had a strong online presence, providing Cole with the distraction he needed.

Minsk had kept an active blog and Facebook account, and he'd contributed to a few dozen online articles about property development. Eventually, the deluge of information was enough to refocus Cole on the case.

Unfortunately, two pots of coffee and eight hours later, Cole had learned nothing about Minsk that was useful in understanding why he had been killed.

"Any luck?" Rita's soft voice and vanilla scent immediately brightened the room.

She shuffled into the living room wearing white cotton shorts and a Rivertown T-shirt. Her mussed hair hung over both shoulders in loose, unkempt waves he instantly ached to run his fingers through.

"A little," Cole said. He moved into the kitchen and poured her a cup of coffee. "Minsk's maid finally returned my call. Alicia something."

"That's good. Oh, thank you." Rita accepted the mug with a puckered brow. "Why are you wearing your uniform?" She sipped the coffee and sighed.

"Good?"

"Heaven." Her sharp hazel eyes popped wide. "Oh, my goodness. I have to call the office." She scanned the room frantically. "I didn't call off. I just never showed up. What time is it? Where's your clock?"

He lifted his watch. "It's only seven ten. Municipal building doesn't even open until eight, so unless you're leaving someone a voice mail, I think you can relax and enjoy the coffee."

"Right." Rita took another appreciative drink. "I guess I'm still waking up."

"You didn't sleep well?" Cole asked, hoping she hadn't been afraid or uneasy about being there alone with him all night.

"Eventually," she said on a yawn, "but my baby brother wants to use my truck to help a friend move, and he's not buying my stories or excuses about why he can't use it. I fielded his interrogative texts until after midnight when I finally insisted he knock it off so I could get some rest before work this morning." She rubbed her forehead. "I just keep lying to him, and that's not who we are. Ryan and I made a pact when he came to live with me. We promised to always be straight with one another."

"You don't want him to use your truck because whoever tried to run you down could mistake him for you in your vehicle," Cole guessed.

"Exactly." Rita dropped her hand and took a long curious look at Cole. "Why are you dressed for work so early?"

"I'm meeting the maid at Mr. Minsk's house in an hour."

Rita blanched. "An hour?" She wrinkled her nose. "All right. I can be ready in ten minutes."

Cole smiled.

"Good. I told West I'd bring you to the station while I interviewed the maid."

"No!" Rita started, nearly spilling her coffee. "I only agreed to go to the station today because I'd be with you. You can't just leave me alone there. What if the killer is a friend or relative of one of the deputies? That would give him access to the jacket and the station. What if he turns up to kill me again and you're not there?" She spun in place and headed back down the hall to his room.

"Where are you going?" Cole called. "Rita?" He followed her as far as the closed door. "Are you mad? Is this a protest?" *What was happening?* Cole latched his fingers behind his head and stared at the ceiling. "I know you're scared, but you've got to trust me or I can't protect you. At least trust my judgment. You will always be safe with my brother." He moved his eyes back to the door. "And don't walk away when we're talking. This is ridiculous."

The door whipped open a moment later.

Rita had swapped her pajamas for dark jeans and a

red V-neck sweater. "I'm going with you." She raked a brush through her hair as she headed for the bathroom and began to brush her teeth. "Just because we didn't see the guy from the coffee shop in the criminal database last night doesn't mean he isn't a criminal."

She spoke around the busy brush and load of toothpaste bubbles. "It only means he doesn't have a record. And just because he wasn't in your personal photos doesn't mean he isn't somehow in your circle. So I'm coming to Minsk's place. I'll wait in the car while you talk to the maid. Then you can take me to the station to make a formal statement afterward." She finished up and checked her face in the mirror. "I want to be where you are." A swipe of lip gloss and some eyelash stuff later, she turned puppy eyes on Cole.

Cole processed her demands.

He didn't like taking her out on a call with him, but knowing she was afraid to be without him, even at the sheriff's department, gave Cole a deep ache in his chest.

"Please?"

He rocked back on his heels. "Fine."

"Thank you!" She perked up.

"Don't forget to call off work."

"Right." Rita grabbed her little purple phone off the counter and pecked the screen before pressing it to her ear. Sixty seconds later, she'd delivered the world's worst performance over voice mail, complete with dry coughing and a gratuitous moan. According to Rita, she'd be out the rest of the week.

Cole hoped to have eliminated the threat against her

well before that, but he wasn't opposed to having a little extra time with her afterward.

He'd protect her.

She'd learn to trust him. Maybe even see past whatever she might have heard about his usual dating style. Not that he was looking to date Rita.

Was he looking to date Rita?

"Are you ready?" she asked, sliding her feet into little white sneakers.

Not even close, he thought wryly. "Yep. I'll give West a call on our way. Let him know there's been a change of plans."

"Really?" Rita's sharp hazel eyes went soft with relief.

"Come on." Cole opened the front door and held it for her to pass.

The right thing for protocol and the right thing for Rita were in opposition at the moment, and it put him in a tough place. With any luck, no other conflicts like this one would come up, because, given the choice, Cole had a feeling he'd always choose Rita. "Let's go before I change my mind."

The snaking hillside road to Minsk's house wound its way past a smattering of high-end homes overlooking the town. Minsk's property was unapologetically larger than the rest and situated at the top of the mountain, stark white against the towering evergreens and surrounded by an elaborate garden with a wrought-iron fence.

"Good grief," Rita said, leaning forward in her seat

as Cole maneuvered the cruiser onto the broad circular drive. "I had no idea this was up here."

A middle-aged woman in traditional gray-and-white servant's attire bustled through the arching ten-foot door before Cole could shift into Park.

He twisted his hat onto his head and gave Rita a warning look. "Wait here."

She rested back against the seat and crossed her arms.

A moment later, he offered the dark-haired woman a handshake and what he hoped was a comforting smile. "You must be Mrs. Sanchez." Her wide brown eyes and olive skin reminded him of his mother's best friend, Anita. Their accents were slightly different, but there was warmth and kindness in both women's eyes.

"I'm so glad you're here," she said. "Please, come." She hustled him inside and shut the door.

The home was enormous. The Garrett boys could've played a nice game of catch in the foyer alone. What would one man do in a house so big? Not that Cole didn't value nice things. He did, but he was also beginning to realize how deeply blessed he was to be surrounded by family and friends. "Thank you for agreeing to meet with me, and for your willingness to meet here."

"He's been gone three days." She lifted the corresponding number of fingers on one hand and shook them.

"Yes, ma'am. I'm sorry we weren't able to find him sooner. The sheriff stopped by twice to check on him, but there was no answer. He'd hoped Mr. Minsk was on a business trip."

"Oh, no," she said. "He was working here. All the time. No rest. No sleep. Then, poof. He was gone."

"Did he keep a home office?" Cole asked. He knew all about the demands of a high-pressure career and lack of everything else that came along with it. "I'd like to take a look at his private calendar and personal computer, as well."

"Of course." She started up a sweeping staircase. "This way."

Cole followed her into a surprisingly plain room with understated furniture and a desk covered in messy files. He lifted the lid on a compact computer. "Is this his only laptop?"

"Yes. He used it all the time. That and his cell phone." Her voice cracked, and she cupped her hands over her mouth.

Cole swiped a finger over the touchpad, and the computer's screen flickered to life. No file icons on the desktop. A quick pass through the drives came up empty, as well. The device was like brand-new. Nothing personal. No history. Strange for a man who'd allegedly used it all the time. Unless… "Have you touched this since he went missing?"

"No, sir."

"Has anyone else been here?"

"Not that I'm aware of," she said, shrugging, "but I only come twice a week."

"Did you notice any signs that Mr. Minsk might've had company in between your visits?"

She raised her shoulders again.

Cole turned his attention back to the clean laptop.

Could Minsk have known he was in danger and cleared his files to protect himself? If so, what was he hiding? And from who?

Cole set the laptop aside. He rummaged through the piles of papers, wondering where to begin. There was no way to do the job justice with Rita waiting in the car. "I'm afraid I'm going to need to get some help in here." He looked up to catch the maid's eye. "We'll have to go through everything in detail." Beneath the mountains of documentation was a solid wood desk. No giant paper calendar like Cole had hoped. Of course not. Minsk was a wealthy businessman. He probably kept all his appointments on a cell phone.

Cole took a photo of the cluttered desk and sent it to West. Sorting the mess could take all day. He definitely needed help. Before that, he needed to get Rita to the sheriff's department. She'd be safe there while he investigated. Uneasy, he knew, but safe.

He teetered a moment, torn between needing to leave and needing to stay. A set of blueprints caught his attention near the bottom of one haphazard pile. Cole worked the papers free and carefully uncurled the edges. It was hard to say what he was looking at without context. "Do you have any idea what Mr. Minsk was working on?" he asked Mrs. Sanchez, still positioned at the office door.

She shifted foot to foot. "No. He didn't talk to me like that, but he was a nice man."

He analyzed her troubled stance and unwillingness to enter the room with him. "Are you uncomfortable for some reason?"

"It doesn't feel right watching you snoop through his things. I know he's gone and you're helping but…"

Cole relaxed by a fraction. "I know it's hard, but I appreciate your help."

He turned his eyes back to the scrolled paperwork before him. What was this blueprint for?

Rita said she'd seen Mr. Minsk at the courthouse several times recently. He could have been buying or negotiating a land deal, or researching a property for a buyer. Maybe the blueprint was related to the property, but which parcel and who was the owner?

Mrs. Sanchez kneaded her hands. "Why would something like this happen to such a nice person?"

"I don't know," Cole admitted, "but I intend to find out."

He gave the wiped laptop another long look.

Was Mr. Minsk as nice a guy as his housekeeper thought? Or was he something else? A few days ago, Cole would've said nice guys weren't shot in the head and dumped in the river, but what did that theory say about Rita? Maybe good people were simply in the wrong place at the wrong time on occasion, and Minsk had been one of them. Like Rita.

He spread the plans on the desk and turned them around twice, trying to make heads or tails of the thin lines and chicken-scratch writing. "This looks like the docks." He lowered his face to the awful handwriting along one edge. "Willa. Eleven o'clock."

The maid moved reluctantly into the room. "Mr. Minsk spent a lot of time on the water."

"Does the name Willa mean anything to you? Was she a business partner? Family member? Girlfriend?"

"No. *Willa* is his boat."

He spent a lot of time on the water. And at the courthouse.

There had been talk of revitalizing the docks for years, but nothing had ever come of it. Maybe Minsk had been trying to make that happen.

Maybe, if Minsk spent a lot of time on his boat, there would be some clues there to help Cole decipher who had killed him and why.

He stared at the blueprint, hoping for the details to snap together, reveal something more than he could yet see.

The ringing of the doorbell turned Mrs. Sanchez into the hallway. "Excuse me," she called over her shoulder, already on her way to the door.

Cole went to the window and pulled back the curtain from the window overlooking Minsk's driveway. His cruiser was empty. The rest of the view was strikingly peaceful.

Was he taking too long, so she'd lost patience, or had she gotten spooked? Either way, he'd known better than to agree to bring her along, and he and Rita would need to have a discussion about what *wait in the car* meant.

Cole rubbed a rough hand over his face, waiting for her voice in the hallway. He needed to get going, anyway. West wanted Rita at the station. Someone else would have to handle Minsk's messy office. He dialed West, then rested a hip against the disorganized desk.

"Where are you?" West answered without greeting.

"I've got stuff to do, and I'm down here sitting on my thumbs waiting for you and Rita Horn to show up."

"We're on the way. I stopped at Minsk's house to talk with the maid first. I've got a paperwork catastrophe over here, but I found a blueprint in the mix that might be useful."

"If you're at Minsk's, where's Rita?" West's flat tone was as disapproving as they came. "Tell me you didn't take our only witness to the murder victim's home."

"She agreed to wait in the car." Cole listened to the gonging silence of the cavernous home. His gut fisted with warning. It was time to collect Rita and get moving. "We're headed your way now, but it sounds like Minsk had a boat at the marina. Could be something there that sheds some light. Someone ought to check that out, as well."

"Agreed, now get your witness down here."

The echo of a single gunshot rang through the massive home.

Cole freed his sidearm, a bullet of fear lancing his heart. He crept toward the open office door and peered down the long hallway. Years of military and department training snapped into focus.

"Was that a gunshot?" West asked. His tight voice burst through the forgotten cell phone on Cole's shoulder.

"Shh." Cole hastened toward the staircase. The view from the second-floor balcony coiled his gut. "Maid's down. Single GSW to the head." A pool of blood seeped around her raven hair on the white marble floor. A lump formed in Cole's throat as the image of his empty cruiser thudded back to mind. "Rita's missing." He disconnected without waiting for West's response.

He shoved the phone into his pocket and took the stairs on silent feet. A near-feral need to protect her burned through his limbs. If Rita was hurt in any way, someone was going to be extremely sorry.

A second shot erupted before he reached the foyer, ringing Cole's ears and shattering the window behind his head.

He dropped into a crouch and pressed his back to the wall. "Cade County Sheriff's Department," Cole announced. "Put your weapon down and come out where I can see you."

Three more rounds exploded in immediate succession, following Cole down the steps and trashing the column where he ducked for cover.

Across the open room, a lean man in a bulky coat dashed out of sight.

Cole gave chase, gun drawn, desperate for a chance to take the shot and terrified he'd find Rita in the same condition he'd found the maid.

RITA PRESSED HERSELF behind a stout hedge at the property's edge, leaving only a few inches between her shaking toes and a ragged cliff. She hadn't seen the man in the deputy coat since he'd manifested from the bushes and rung the bell to the house, but she'd counted four gunshots so far.

How he'd missed seeing her in the car was both a miracle and a mystery.

She'd ducked on instinct, huddling into the shadowed

space between her seat and the dashboard, praying the killer wouldn't take undo interest in Cole's cruiser.

The first gunshot had set her upright.

The second had propelled her out of hiding.

The third and fourth shots had rooted her feet in place behind the shrubbery as if she was part of the garden.

Cole was still inside, and she wouldn't leave without him.

Tears streamed over her cheeks as she imagined the killer sneaking up on Cole and pulling the trigger while she hid like a coward. She begged her limbs to cooperate and carry her back to the car where she'd stupidly left her phone in the cupholder when she fled. She needed to call for help.

Should she return to the car for her phone? Make a run for the closest neighbor?

Rita leaned around the shrubbery, seeking the nearest home in each direction and estimating which was closer.

"Stop!" Cole's strong voice cracked through the hills.

Her heart leaped in response.

"Come out." Cole moved swiftly in her direction, gun drawn but lowered slightly. He extended a hand to her. "I lost him. I need to get you out of here before he comes back."

Rita shimmied free and grabbed his offered hand in both of hers. "How could you see me?"

"I'm beginning to think I could find you anywhere." Cole cursed under his breath. He pulled her to him and sighed against the top of her head. "Did you see which way the shooter went?"

"No. I haven't seen him since he went inside."

Cole pulled back for a look into Rita's eyes. Confliction danced over his features. "West's on his way. We're going to get in the cruiser and go. Understand? I'm not involving you in a shoot-out."

Cole led her back through the gardens at a crouched jog. "Stay low," he reminded her. "And don't stop."

"Cole!" Rita froze. She yanked him back, gripping his stubborn arm in both her hands.

The shooter had appeared again in the distance.

"It's the man from the Rivertown coffee house." This time, he wore the deputy jacket.

Cole lifted his weapon, scanning the area.

"There," she whispered, wagging one frantic finger. "That's him!"

The man's head turned immediately in their direction. His arm swung forward, gun in hand. The shot cracked in the autumn air.

"Run," Cole barked, shoving Rita aside and positioning his body between her and the gunman. He returned fire as they ran, but stayed tight to Rita's side as far as the cruiser. He yanked the driver's side door open and stuffed Rita inside.

She climbed over the console and into the passenger seat as Cole revved the engine to life. He spun the vehicle in a reverse circle, tossing Rita against her door, and pointed the cruiser back down the winding road at twice the posted speed.

Sirens cried in the distance as Cole relayed details of

the shooting to Dispatch. Apparently he'd been on the phone with West when the first shot rang out.

Her heart hammered against her ribs, threatening to break them. Her stomach knotted, and her hands ached for something to hold. Nothing seemed real. The day had to be a dream. A movie she'd seen years before and nearly forgotten. Anything but reality. This could not be her actual life.

"Rita?" Cole's steady voice seeped into her clouded thoughts. "She's nonresponsive." He traced the line of her arm with careful fingers, then tenderly grazed her shoulder and neck. "I don't see any injuries. She's in shock, I think."

"I'm not," Rita said, jerking her face in his direction.

"Ask West to call me." Cole returned the radio handset to his console, then shifted into Park. He parked the cruiser behind a small white church off the winding road. "Dispatch is taking over. And it's okay to be in shock. It's okay to feel whatever you're feeling. You were shot at. Stalked by an active shooter."

"You saved me."

The corners of Cole's mouth pulled down. "No. I'm the reason you were in danger. You shouldn't have been there. Then you wouldn't have needed saving."

The plea in his tone and determination in his eyes lit a flame in Rita's core. Heat rose and spread from her middle. Cole Garrett was her hero.

Rita unlatched her seatbelt and turned to face him. She raised a palm to the stubble on his cheeks and curled her fingertips against the strong line of his jaw.

Shock flashed in his eyes before quickly becoming

something else. "Rita?" His voice was low and gravelly with want.

"Yes."

Cole reached for her then, winding a strong arm over her back and pulling her toward him until she was on her knees, stretching back across the infuriating console.

Her lips met his in a perfect collision of passion and relief. It was the moment she'd been dreaming of since she'd first set eyes on him all those months ago, and it was everything she'd expected and more. Expert hands lifted her in the confined space of his front seat. Greedy and protective, they brought her gently to rest on his lap.

Rita arranged her thighs over his before deepening the kiss. She towered over him, caressing his face in her hands and eagerly opening her mouth when his tongue swept across her bottom lip, asking for more.

The radio crackled beside them as Dispatch announced the need for another car at Minsk's home.

Cole broke the kiss with a groan, leaving Rita breathless and perched awkwardly over him.

She buried her face in the curve of his neck and tried not to think of how to get back into her seat like a lady. "I am so sorry."

His chest went still. "You attacked me."

Rita reared back. "No."

Cole's mischievous smile washed the wave of humiliation away. "Adrenaline makes people do crazy things."

Rita climbed off his lap much less smoothly than she'd arrived. "I think it was your apology."

"Well, then, I am very, very sorry," he said.

She buckled her seatbelt with a grin, hating the rush of heat across her cheeks. "Shut up."

Chapter Nine

Cole pulled back onto the curving country road, his grip tight on the steering wheel. What was he thinking? Kissing her like that. Letting the heat of the moment burn through his professionalism.

Rita gazed out the window, likely regretting the way she'd kissed him or the fact she'd let him drag her onto his lap like they were people who made out in cars instead of what they were. Practically strangers, on the run from a killer.

Correction. Rita was on the run. Cole was on the hunt, and at his first opportunity, Cole would bring this guy down.

Cole's cell phone rang, and he hit speaker. "Garrett."

"Hey," West answered. "I'm at Minsk's. Where are you?"

"Headed to the marina. I think we need to get eyes on that boat before someone else gets to it. If they haven't already."

West sighed heavily. Cole could practically hear him aging. "And Rita?"

"She's here. You're on speaker."

A beat of awkward silence filled the car.

"Hi," Rita said shyly, wrinkling her brow and locking her gaze on Cole.

Cole smiled at the silly look. "Any sign of the shooter?"

"No," West answered, "but we've got a vehicle with no plates around the curve past the house. We're checking it out."

"Black sedan?" Cole asked.

"No. Silver hatchback."

Rita deflated against the passenger seat, allowing her head to roll aside.

"Keep me posted," Cole said. "We'll meet you at the station afterward."

"Sounds good."

Cole tossed the phone into a cupholder and hooked the next right toward the river. He examined Rita's expressionless profile. "If the shooter's anywhere near Minsk's house, West will find him. West's one of the best trackers I know, and the other deputies are diligent. If the shooter isn't long gone by now, he'll never make it."

Rita's face went slack, as if a horrible thought had just occurred to her. "The maid," she whispered.

"I know." Cole lifted a hand to comfort her, but returned it to the wheel. The maid's death was his fault. He should've been with her. He was the one who'd invited her there. And damn if he didn't feel like he'd been one step behind Minsk's killer from the moment he'd laid eyes on his body being dragged from the river. Cole couldn't keep doing this. He had to get ahead of the sonofabitch before Rita was next to pay the price.

A pair of fat tears slid over her cheeks. "He killed her," she said. "For what? Answering the door? What about her family? She could have a husband. Children." The final word was barely a sound on her tongue.

Cole's heart ached for hers. "I'm sorry." Rita had lost her mom senselessly, too. He couldn't imagine what this day felt like to her.

"She shouldn't have been a part of this."

"You're right." And he hated himself for asking the poor woman to meet him at Minsk's home. Cole had wanted her there to provide insight into the man he'd never met. He'd never imagined…

"What happens now?" Rita asked in a small, heart-broken voice. "Who will tell her family?"

"West." Cole answered mindlessly. These were the things his big brother insisted on handling. *My county. My people. My responsibility*, he'd say. "He'll deliver the news and answer whatever questions he can for them. Then, he'll set his sights on the killer and won't stop going for him until justice is done."

Though Cole planned to beat him to it this time.

Eventually, they left the shaded mountain pass in favor of a sprawling two-lane highway that stretched for miles between sun-drenched cornfields. Several raggedy scarecrows and the occasional combine peppered the landscape before they reached the river. Cole flipped his signal and gave the new road a long look. A mile to the east, hidden beyond the curve of a rolling hillside, stood a number of abandoned factories, homeless cats and a recent murder site. Cole drove west, toward Memorial Park, wide waterfront homes and a beautifully landscaped marina.

He pulled the receiver off his dashboard and held it to his lips. "I'm at the Cade County Marina. Checking in." He released the handset and waited.

"Roger that," a grainy voice returned.

Cole made a slow circle around the nearly empty lot before choosing a space and settling the engine. He released his seatbelt and turned his face to Rita, unsure what to say. If he asked her to join him, he might unintentionally lead her onto a boat with a gunman. Though the alternative seemed equally dangerous, he'd already resolved not to let her out of his sight again.

"Ready?" He tipped his head toward the windshield, indicating the row of boats bobbing outside.

She didn't need a second invitation. Rita hustled around the car's hood to meet him. "What are we looking for?"

"Minsk's boat. *Willa*." Cole pointed to a line of red block letters on the closest fishing vessel.

"Got it." Rita kept pace at his side, reading the name of each boat softly as they passed.

A long whistle blew over Cole's lips when he spotted her. *Willa* wasn't a boat, she was a yacht. Coming from Minsk's mansion on the mountain, Cole shouldn't have been surprised, but he was. The largest boat he'd been on outside the military was a historic schooner near Williamsburg. This vessel was something else entirely. Definitely not a fishing boat. *Willa* was seventy-five feet of luxury, from her shining metal rails to her spotless wide-planked deck. "Looks like we've arrived."

Cole kicked a set of freestanding wooden steps across the dock toward *Willa* before stretching one long leg out and pulling himself completely on board. "Your turn." He reached for Rita, who easily accepted his hand. Color flooded her face, and his chest puffed at the response.

He couldn't ignore the way her smaller, softer palm fit perfectly into his larger one, or the way she willingly gripped him back. Maybe she didn't regret their kiss as much as he'd feared. Maybe she liked how their hands, and earlier their mouths, had melded together as much as he did.

What he refused to think about, for now, was how nicely she'd fit across his lap, and how much nicer that could've been without the car and several layers of clothes. A rush of electricity flowed over his skin as her body pressed briefly against his for balance.

"Oops." She released his hand in favor of bracing both palms on his chest to find her footing.

Cole caught her at the curves of her waist. "Okay?"

She dropped her arms to her sides and stepped away. "Yeah."

Cole closed his fingers into fists, hating the loss of her nearness. "Let's see what *Willa* knows."

RITA FOLLOWED COLE through the small cabin door, the feel of his hands still warming her waist. She wet her lips, relishing the tingle left behind from the gentle scrape of his stubble. It was only her imagination that insisted her lips were still flavored with the taste of his tongue.

"You okay?" he asked, clearing her hazy thoughts.

"Yes." She moved into the boat's broad gathering space and paused at Cole's side, arms crossed over her middle in a useless attempt to settle her churning nerves and butterflies.

Cole worked methodically through the piles of clutter on a desk in the corner, then moved to a pile of folders on a nearby credenza.

Rita took in the impressive surroundings. The boat was bigger than some of the apartments her family had lived in while following her dad across the country. Military communities were tight, and there were no secrets, as much by necessity as choice. She'd begun to miss those simpler days since coming home to find her house ransacked. That wouldn't have happened if all her neighbors were soldiers.

She took a few cautious steps around a protruding bar, eager for a better look at the fancy dining area behind it. An oval-shaped table was positioned in the corner and wrapped by bench seating. White china and stemmed glasses were arranged on the table, waiting for a meal that would never come. Piles of lavish pillows covered in rich shades of blue and gold silk buried the narrow bank of seats.

Rita trailed her fingertips over the delicate fabric before moving away. She peeked through small round windows at the distant horizon where dark waters met green mountains and a clear blue sky.

"Bingo," Cole announced.

Rita headed back immediately. "What did you find?" Her pulse raced in anticipation. After the horror she'd seen today, anything seemed possible. Even the things that shouldn't touch her small town. The man in the black sedan. The one who'd murdered two people in two days. He'd changed everything.

Cole spread a blueprint over the messy desk and anchored it at either end with folders. "Look." He took a photo with his phone, then layered another blueprint on top of the first and repeated the process.

Rita leaned closer, one fist pressed to her chest in prayer. *Please don't let these be schematics for a bomb.* A small measure of relief washed over her as she examined the image. "Is that the marina?"

"No, but you're close. This is a stretch of docks on the Mississippi River in New Orleans. I saw a similar blueprint in Minsk's home office. That one looked like our docks. Interesting that he'd have both, don't you think? The Ohio River runs right into the Mississippi River. Two blueprints for properties on the same body of water all these miles apart?"

He peeled back the top paper and waved a hand at the one underneath. "This is a dock in Illinois." He tapped a finger on a line of text along the paper's border. "Confluence with the Ohio River." Cole set his phone down and turned for a final blueprint he'd leaned against the desk's side. He spread it out and took a picture. "And St. Louis." He shook his head, pointing to a similar line of text on this blueprint's edge. "Confluence with the Missouri River."

"I see." Rita struggled to understand the implication. Cole seemed excited over a stack of basic blueprints.

That was Minsk's job, wasn't it? "We knew Minsk was a land developer. Maybe he developed docks."

Cole rolled each blueprint carefully and fed them into one another until he had only one thick roll to carry. "Yes, but this information could be very useful in figuring what Minsk was up to before he died. For example, if there's been any bids made on our docks, we can follow that up as a lead, or if the same company has purchased all the other properties, that's worth hunting, too."

Well, put that way, the blueprints sounded like progress. "It's a shame Minsk didn't live long enough to see our docks sold," Rita said. "I remember the explosion that killed four workers there. It was a hot topic the year I moved to town."

Cole turned slowly to face her. "I'd almost forgotten about that. My family attended the memorial service for the fallen workers."

"Me, too," she said. It had been a case she'd followed closely. A major catastrophe only months after she'd moved to Rivertown for school, away from her family, alone in a tiny apartment with a view of the fires that had burned through the night, searing oil patches released into the river by the explosion. She'd carried bottled water and sandwiches to workers for days as they dragged the river in search of the four bodies. Seen the missing men's loved ones sobbing on the riverbanks.

"All four families filed lawsuits, and the company was eventually foreclosed on. The lawyers had proved it was a preventable explosion, and the company couldn't afford the settlement. A ton of families lost their jobs when that place went out of business. It was a mess. The grieving families didn't mean to hurt anyone else. They just wanted to be sure the company didn't let anyone else die."

Cole fixed her with his sharp blue eyes. "I wonder who owns it now. If not the company who went bankrupt, then who?"

Rita shrugged. "The state was supposed to buy it and make it into a memorial honoring those families, but it never happened." She puffed air into thick side-swept bangs, wincing at the reminder of her swollen forehead. "That's how it goes sometimes. Politicians make promises to pacify the people until the heat blows over, then the vows are forgotten." The lost were forgotten. The families… She rubbed her eyes, erasing images of the makeshift memorial created by neighbors for her mother following the crash.

Rita pulled in long breaths and plucked the material of her shirt away from her chest. The air inside the cabin was too stuffy. Claustrophobic. Grief was powerful enough without adding it to the day she was having. She swallowed long and hard to clear her thickening throat and refocused on the docks. "There was going to be a boardwalk with benches that had the lost men's names on little plaques, and locally owned businesses, like ice cream shops and fishing pole rentals. Instead, it's just a big ugly reminder of an avoidable tragedy." And haven to seventeen cats.

Cole's phone buzzed on the desk where it had been acting as a paperweight. "Garrett," he answered, tucking the rolled blueprints under one arm. He flicked his gaze to Rita then back to the desk. "Yeah." He pulled a stack of files toward him, shifting the pages and stacking them up. "Are you sure?" His body stiffened. "We're on our way." He stuffed the phone into his pocket and fixed Rita with sincere blue eyes. "West says they still haven't found the shooter, but someone cleared out Minsk's office while West and the team were tracking the killer through the woods. The coroner was in the foyer downstairs and never heard a thing."

Fear lifted Rita's skin into gooseflesh. "Then this guy's really good. That's very bad."

"Yeah, and he's bold as hell." Cole stacked files ten tall into his hands and rested his chin on the top to steady them. "Grab what you can. We'll come back with help. For now, we need to go."

Rita obeyed, pulling photos from the corkboard over the desk and stacking them on piles of folders as large as her short arms could manage.

A small thud registered in the cabin. Something had fallen on the silent deck beyond the little door. It reminded Rita of the sound made when a package was delivered to her porch.

Except they were on a boat.

"What was that?" she finally asked, half afraid to know the answer.

Cole set the files back on the desk, then unlatched the button securing his sidearm to its holster. "Stay here." He crept silently up the stairs.

Rita followed on his heels, unable to sit still again and wait to be abducted or killed.

Cole swiveled at the waist. He gripped a fist in the

air and grimaced. It was the military signal for *stand down. Don't move. Wait.*

Rita had seen the move many times before, and somehow, the visual command was impossible for her to ignore. Her feet froze on the small set of steps to the little door.

Cole shoved the door wide, gun drawn and ready. A string of fervent curses bit the air.

Before he could bark another order, Rita's eyes landed on a small black device near Cole's feet. Bright red numbers counted backward toward zero. The soft ticking of a clock registering with each change on the display. *17, 16, 15...*

Rita gasped. "Is that a bomb?"

Papers fluttered through the air as Cole tossed the stack of folders from her hands toward the dock. He swung back to face her, this time gripping her wrists and tugging her up the steps toward him.

Rita's feet bumbled forward, catching each rung on autopilot while she stared, transfixed by the device that would end her too-short life.

9, 8, 7...

He yanked her arms, dragging her away from the device when she landed on deck beside it, but her body didn't respond.

"Rita!" Cole yelled, his voice thick with demand and authority. "Move your ass before I throw you overboard."

6, 5, 4...

Her brother would be all alone. An orphan without a sister to watch over him. Abandoned by everyone because his stupid bleeding-heart sister, the only thing he had left, had to feed cats at a murder location.

Something gripped her mercilessly, and she winced with the shock of pain that followed. A powerful jerk hoisted her off her feet and hefted her into the air. Rita's arms flew wide as she sailed away from the boat and crashed painfully into the now-choppy river like an anvil. Her eyes stung and her lungs burned as she broached the surface a moment later, swallowing mouthfuls of disgusting, frigid river water in the process.

Cole followed immediately, launching himself over the polished chrome rail. His arms were around her in the next second, forcing her farther from the boat with each powerful thrust of his legs. He made a show of filling his cheeks with air, then dunked them both underwater.

The explosion that followed shoved them through the water in a powerful undertow. They resurfaced to chaos. Her teeth rattled and her vision blurred. Heat scorched over the river in an invisible wave, and Cole curved himself around her like a shield, pressing her face against his chest and wrapping her in his iron arms.

Smoke plumed and billowed overhead. Debris dropped from the sky and floated around them in a rancid stew of scorched plastic and burning fuel. Rita coughed and hacked, kicking instinctively to stay above water as fragments of torn metal and burning planks shot into the water like missiles.

"Are you okay?" Cole asked, petting Rita's hair and dragging it away from her skin for a closer look at her nonexistent injuries.

"I'm fine. I'm sorry," she cried. "I didn't move. I should've moved." He'd saved her life. Again. Her heart welled with emotion, and she gripped his handsome face in both palms.

The shadow of something large barely registered with her before crashing over them.

"Cole!" But her cry was too late.

The still-burning debris landed across his broad shoulders with a sickening crack.

His handsome face went slack, and his protective grip on her released.

Chapter Ten

Rita caught hold of the dock with one hand as she struggled to keep Cole above water. One hand wrapped under his arm, she pressed her cheek to his.

Cole's eyes flashed open. Shock and confusion raked his brow.

"Be still," she warned through trembling lips. "I don't know how hurt you are."

He began to tread water slowly, attempting to shift away from her. "Are you okay?" His voice was rough and low, his face pinched in pain.

The precious sound was nearly enough to push her under. She pressed her forehead to his and let her tears fall on his cheeks. "I'm perfect," she cried, and it was true.

Cole Garrett's presence in her life had changed everything, and she never again wanted to go a day without him in it. Ten thousand words lodged in her throat and on her tongue, but she could only pull back for a better look at his face and state the obvious. "Be still. You're hurt."

The pounding footfalls of marina workers and nearby

boat owners soon rattled the dock. Life preservers and rescue ropes were lowered into Cole's and Rita's reach. A mass of voices churned the acrid air. Moments blurred and time elapsed in a surreal and unsettling way as Rita was pulled from the water by the careful hands of a dozen men.

Cole insisted on climbing out unassisted.

Rita watched the remains of the flaming boat in disbelief. Had she really stood in the below-deck cabin only minutes before? Had someone nearly blown her up?

The distant, lamenting cry of an ambulance wound into a frenzy at the marina's main entrance, then stopped just short of mowing her over in the name of rescue.

Newly arriving deputies and marina security corralled the hodgepodge rescue team and detained them for questioning behind a flimsy line of yellow tape. The ambulance workers had divided themselves between Rita and Cole. Rita got the younger, friendlier one. Cole got a familiar-looking man, at least fifteen years his senior. Rita's guy gave her a quick once-over and an oxygen mask. She was fine. Thanks to Cole.

The other guy's job wasn't nearly as easy. Cole's complaints had started at the sight of him and persisted with fervor. "Knock it off!"

"Hold still," the medic snapped. "I'd be done by now if you'd stop fighting me, or didn't you learn that in medical school."

"I'm fine." Cole wiggled on the ambulance's shiny silver bumper. He was far too large for the seat he'd chosen, but had refused the gurney and all attempts to get him to go into the vehicle willingly.

"Good thing you quit school," the man snarked, dabbing Cole's back with sopping cotton pads. "They'd have kicked you out eventually if you're dumb enough to think people are fine after a bombing and near drowning."

Rita smiled through another round of Cole's fervent cursing, glad he was alive and thankful the medic was ignoring his protests. Her ringing ears made it hard to understand everything he said, but she got the gist.

She tried not to think about the moment Cole's eyes had fallen shut and his limbs had gone limp. The sickening curl of her gut was something she never wanted to feel again.

Firemen blasted the charred remains of Minsk's boat and walked the dock, taking pictures and scribbling on clipboards.

Rita refocused on breathing in the sweet oxygen from her mask and blowing out the terror that had constricted her lungs and throat more often than not over the last thirty-six hours.

Beside her, the paramedic continued to mumble as he worked over Cole's battered skin.

Cole swatted the man's hands away. "Leave it!"

The older man sucked his teeth and pressed on, cleaning the burns and wounds across Cole's scarred back. "Hold still and suck it up. Let me do my job. You know, you could try being thankful you've still got breath to complain with."

Cole's gaze lifted to Rita's.

She offered a small smile, tugging the blessed oxygen mask away from her face to speak. Her throat ached with emotion, still raw from her cries for help. "He's right. You should let him finish." Cole had only been unconscious for a few seconds, but those moments had felt like consecutive eternities to Rita. The giant hunk of the boat's hull would have killed her if Cole hadn't been there to take the blow. Protecting her at any cost. Guilt clawed her heart, but darned if his bravery wasn't sexy as hell. It had been a long while since anyone other than her baby brother had played the role of her protector.

The fact that Cole probably thought he was just doing his job soured the moment. She did her best to mask the sudden disappointment.

"See?" the medic said. "Listen to her. Maybe she should go to medical school."

Rita smiled. "Besides, if any of that gets infected, you'll have all new reasons to swear."

Cole turned his frowning face toward the water without any more argument.

The paramedic gave Cole a long look before casting Rita a curious grin. "Well, well, well."

"No," Cole said. "None of that." He jerked his shoulder away from the man's touch and shot him a warning look. "Just patch me up so I can get back to work."

The sharp bark of a siren set Cole on his feet, immediately free from the medic's reach. "About damn time."

West appeared at the dock's end, running full speed toward them.

Reporters and spectators moved aside as he hopped the makeshift yellow fence.

He slowed as he drew nearer, both hands anchored to his hips. "What the holy hell happened here?" His growling voice was the perfect mix of fear, relief and outrage. It was the sound of an older sibling whose little brother had been wronged.

Being a big sister, Rita knew that one well. She'd had her *Thank goodness you're okay, now who do I need to flatten?* voice at the ready for nineteen years and counting.

West stopped at her side, flipping his hands into the air. His eyes darted from Cole's scowl to the paramedic's kind eyes. "Well? Uncle Henry?"

Uncle Henry?

"I don't know about the boat," the paramedic started, "but Stanford over here is lucky to be alive. He's got extensive first and second degree burns over most of his back and shoulders, lacerations on the head and neck, multiple contusions—" he made an unintelligible sound "—everywhere. No signs of a concussion, despite the temporary loss of consciousness after being clocked on the head with a hunk of the flaming hull." He shrugged. "I want to take him to the hospital for a thorough exam."

"Cole?" West asked, arms crossed, brows furrowed. "No."

Uncle Henry lifted his palms, looking exactly like his nephew had a minute prior. "Tell your mama I tried."

"Always do," West said. He embraced the older man briefly. "Thanks, Uncle Henry."

"Don't thank me." Henry tipped his head in Rita's direction. "He blacked out in the water. This one pulled him to the dock and kept him afloat until help arrived."

Rita's face heated. "He threw me off the boat when I was too scared to move. Then he jumped in and shielded me from the explosion. I'm the reason he's hurt."

West rubbed his forehead. "He's hurt because he should've been a doctor."

Cole groaned. "I didn't want to be a damn doctor. Now, if you're all done mothering me, we need to get back to work."

"You're hurt," Henry started. He snapped his mouth shut a moment later and raised his hands in surrender.

"I know," Cole agreed, softening his tone slightly. "I'm cut, burned and bruised, none of which is critical, and we need to focus on what's happening around here. We had a literal boatload of information on Minsk's business and it just went up in flames."

Henry shifted his gaze to Rita and the young paramedic at her side. "Your patient doing better than mine?"

"Yes, sir. Some minor abrasions, smoke inhalation, probably a lifelong aversion to watercraft, but she'll be fine."

Henry bobbed his head and swung his attention back to Cole, a growing look of pride on his face. "Good work, deputy." He slapped Cole's shoulder, then winced. "Sorry."

Cole gritted his teeth until his face was as red as his back.

"Take this." Henry handed Cole a clean, dry T-shirt. "I want it back, so don't get any ideas about keeping it."

West closed in on Cole.

Henry delivered a pile of first aid supplies to Rita.

"For my nephew's burns. See if you can get him to change the bandages twice a day and take something for pain." He dumped the packages into her palms, then unhooked her oxygen mask. "Good luck." He marched back to his ambulance and swung himself inside. His sidekick followed.

Rita stared at the creams and bandages. *Back to being somebody's keeper.* Trusting someone else to call the shots had been nice while it lasted, but at least caretaking was a role she understood, unlike how to be the target of a psychopath, for example. She took a seat on the dock and piled the supplies at her side. Yesterday had been rock-bottom bad, but today was unfathomably worse.

She slumped forward, resting tired forearms against her thighs. Her skin and clothes smelled like dirty river water and burned hair. No amount of soap would ever remove it.

"Everything's completely destroyed," Cole complained behind her. "The files. Blueprints. Everything. I took some pictures to send to you, but now my phone is at the bottom of the river."

West sauntered closer to the smoldering husk of Minsk's boat. "Two shootings in two days. A bomb on a boat." Disappointment colored his cheeks and frustration sharpened his words. "What's happening to my county?"

Rita pressed her eyes shut. A lunatic had also chased her down the crowded street of a college town and forced her headfirst into an historic fountain, but she didn't think West needed to be reminded of that right now. She peeled stinging eyes open and concentrated on being alive. Whatever else happened, she'd try not to think too hard about the angry look on Cole's face when he'd awoken in her arms.

COLE WATCHED RITA drift away from them, choosing to sit alone on the dock several feet away rather than stand in their little huddle and listen to him gripe any longer. Not that he blamed her. He wasn't his biggest fan at the moment, either. Throwing her from the boat and shielding her from the explosion was supposed to be heroic. Maybe even epic. It should have been the kind of story he'd relish telling his future grandkids, but instead, he'd become the one in need of rescue.

Rita had saved Cole's life.

Dammit.

"Don't forget the car in Rivertown," Cole grouched. "He tried to run her down on a crowded street in broad daylight."

West's long-winded ramble about the last few days' events was true, but incomplete. He'd forgotten one of the scariest things Cole had ever seen. "The nut nearly killed her in front of a hundred college kids."

Rita shot him a look over one shoulder. The disappointment in her expression was a perfect match for Cole's current feelings. "I can't believe everything's gone," she said. "I'm trying to be thankful we survived, but it really stinks that all those files are a total loss."

Cole agreed. He scanned the gathering crowd of nosy locals and news crews. More than one set of male eyes watched Rita as she plucked river-drenched fabric away from her skin, where it had become somewhat transparent.

He moved into the onlookers' line of sight and returned their stares until they found something other than Rita to gawk at. He turned back to her a moment later, satisfied by his success.

Rita squinted up at him and smiled.

Heat spread through his core, warming him until his chest burned with the same intensity as his back. A sneaky realization poked its way into his thoughts. His irritation with those rubberneckers had nothing to do with protecting a traumatized woman from their stares and everything to do with protecting *this* woman, *his woman*, from their stares. *Dammit.*

Cole rolled his shoulders uselessly, hating the unfamiliar knotting of his muscles and the setting of his jaw. He was jealous. Of strangers. He hadn't been bothered by this particular emotion since high school. He didn't like it then, and he downright hated it now.

Not to mention, he had no business feeling anything personal for Rita Horn. She was a citizen in need of temporary protection and nothing more. Once the threat to her was eliminated, she'd go back to her life in progress, probably glad to be rid of a man who'd toss her in the river, then force her to keep him afloat or watch him drown.

Humiliation knotted in his chest.

He flicked his attention to West, who'd gone the length of Minsk's boat and back, apparently still in disbelief. "Hey."

Concern dragged West's brows into a deep V. "Yeah."

"Before it blew up, that boat had a bunch of blueprints for other waterfront locations like our docks. All the way from Louisiana to Missouri. Any chance you've had time to find out who Minsk was seeing at the municipal building?"

West's wrinkled forehead went flat. "No. I was pulled off that hunt when someone took a shot at you over at our first victim's house. I couldn't find that shooter, but I did find another body about thirty minutes before you were nearly blown up, and now I'm here wondering who's trying to kill you."

Rita bent her knees and hugged them to her chest. "Maybe the bomber wasn't trying to kill anyone," she said.

West hiked an eyebrow and gave what was left of the boat a pointed look.

"I thought so, too, at first," Rita said, lifting a hand to her forehead as she squinted against the sun. "But look at this mess." She waved her free hand at the bits of charred wreckage floating in the water and scraps of torched paper blowing over the dock. "Maybe this was just about getting rid of evidence."

"With a bomb?" West asked.

She shrugged. "I'm just saying. If the shooter came here to kill us, he could've opened the door and gotten the job done with a lot less noise. We know a handgun is his weapon of choice. Why change attack methods so drastically? He could have taken his shot while we walked to or from the boat if he didn't want to climb aboard and look for us. Honestly, I don't think anyone knew we were in there."

West pinned Cole with a meaningful stare.

Rita could be right.

"Cole?" Rita shifted onto her hands and knees, staring intently between the wooden boards beneath her. "Look."

Cole crouched to follow her gaze. "What?"

"It's the pen!" She crawled over the ash-littered deck, keeping close tabs on something bobbing in the water below them. "Why did you have it with you? That was our only evidence! It might have had the killer's fingerprints!"

West dropped into view at Cole's side. "Evidence?"

"The pen," she gasped, stretching an arm off the opposite side of the dock. Dark locks of wet hair clung to her cheeks and neck. "Help!" She scooted on her belly, attempting to reach a bobbing portion of the silver metal in the water.

"Careful." Cole grabbed Rita's hips before she spilled back into the water. Pain licked his neck and shoulders, fresh cuts and burns protesting the sudden move. "That's not the one you gave me."

"What pen?" West asked. His long shadow wobbled on the waves.

"Got it." Rita backed herself onto the boards beside him. "It's ruined." She held the broken pen daintily between her thumb and forefinger. Heavy tears hung in her sweet hazel eyes. "Why can't one single thing go right for us?"

Cole took a seat at her side. He liked the way she

said "us" a little more than he should. At least he had good news. "The pen you gave me is still locked in the cruiser's glove box. I planned to deliver it into evidence when we went to the station." He hadn't expected the day would take any of the turns it had. Though the kiss they'd shared nearly made up for being shot at.

Rita blew out a long breath. "Oh, thank goodness. So, at least we still have that." She dropped her hands into her lap and leaned her shoulder against his.

West's face popped into view. He squatted before them in sheriff mode "I need to know about the pen. Now, please." He took the impostor pen from Rita's hands and twisted it in half. Where a tube of ink should have been, there was a small metal rectangle attached to the pen's top. "A thumb drive?"

Cole's mind jerked into action. Rita had been right to mistake the item in West's hands for the one she'd given him in a plastic baggie. The two were identical. And if the pen in West's hand was a thumb drive... A smile etched Cole's face. What about the one in his glove box?

Rita was on her feet, pacing before him and waving her hands as she delivered the blow-by-blow to West. "It was just lying there by the blood on the docks the night Minsk was killed, so I put it in my purse. Then I gave it to Cole."

Cole stretched to his full height with a grunt. "Let's go see if all those pens were made equally."

West rolled his shoulders back and took long sheriff-like strides as he led the way to the parking lot.

Cole grabbed Rita's hand and fell in line behind his brother. He laced his fingers with hers and struggled not to limp as he kept pace. "This guy kept a clean laptop. Saved files to secret devices. Hid paperwork on a boat. Makes me think he knew he was in trouble."

West grunted. "Minsk probably thought the files were enough insurance to preserve his life. He was the only one who knew where they were, so in theory, his killer should've had to keep him alive if they wanted the information."

Rita squeezed Cole's hand. "If there are files on that pen and the information is worth stalking me, tossing my house and trying repeatedly to murder me, then I bet the killer's name is one of the things you'll find."

Cole broke into a painful jog, easily bypassing West. He couldn't rewind time and save Minsk, but he could bring the killer to justice and make sure that guy never got anywhere near Rita again.

Chapter Eleven

West held the plastic baggie from Cole's glove box with reverence. "This is the best thing I've seen in days." He handed the precious cargo to Cole while he snapped plastic gloves over his hands. "Here's hoping," he said, peeling the bag open and fishing the pen from its tissue cocoon.

West gripped the device on both ends and twisted. The pieces came easily apart. "Hot damn." Just like the busted pen in the river, this, too, was only a clever disguise for a thumb drive. He raised wide eyes to Cole. "I'm going to deliver this to the lab myself."

"Good idea," Cole agreed. No sense letting the only known piece of evidence out of his sight. Who knew what sort of information Tech Support would find on that tiny drive? "We're going back to my place. We'll meet you at the station after a hot shower and change of clothes."

West slid his eyes in Rita's direction, then back to Cole. "All right. If I'm not there, give me a call. I've still got a crime scene at Minsk's house and that mess over there to deal with." He hooked a thumb toward the capsizing boat.

Cole checked his watch. The face was cracked, but the second hand was ticking. "If I can get there before it closes, I'll swing by the municipal building. Maybe someone knows who Minsk had been visiting. I'd like to know exactly what he was up to during his last few days."

West tucked the baggie into the pocket of his sheriff's coat. "Lots to do. We'd better roll."

Cole nodded goodbye to his brother before opening the passenger door.

Rita inched closer but didn't climb in.

Sparks of electricity charged the air between them, and for a minute, he allowed himself to imagine Rita kissing him again. This time in front of half the gawking town instead of hidden in his car behind an empty church. Maybe she could somehow still see him as a hero, even after she'd had to save him when he blacked out.

Rita kicked the toe of her sodden shoe against the ground, her pretty hazel eyes focused completely on the earth. "I'm sorry you were hurt."

The punch to his chest couldn't have hit any deeper. He'd failed her today, and she was as sorry about it as he was. Before he could find the words to apologize, she dropped into the car and pulled her feet inside.

RITA MENTALLY KICKED herself all the way back to Cole's house. *I'm sorry you were hurt?* Of all the things racing through her mind, *that* was what she'd chosen to say? Worse, he'd looked at her like she'd slapped him when she said it, so she'd avoided speaking for the duration of the drive. Unfortunately, she wouldn't be able to hide much longer.

Cole settled the cruiser's engine in his driveway and climbed out.

This wasn't like a random blind date where she could go home and put her awkward words behind her. She was practically living with Cole, at least until further notice, and he rarely let her out of his sight. After the shoot-out at Minsk's house, she imagined her alone time would be relegated to bathroom breaks.

She hustled onto the porch behind him and waited while he unlocked the door.

Cole ushered her inside and locked up. After a quick sweep of the house, he returned with a stack of dry clothes and a towel. "How about that shower?"

Rita's cheeks heated. She looked away in case he could somehow read the explicit thoughts racing through her mind. "You should go first. You're hurt."

Cole's brows knit together. His mouth curled down. "Please stop saying that."

"Why? You *are* hurt." She crossed her arms to stop the tremor building in her gut. Blood had risen in the water as she kept him afloat. She'd seen the gashes on his shoulders, could only imagine the burns on his back or what it looked like now that Cole's uncle had stitched and cleaned him up. The replacement shirt he'd taken, to keep dirty, river-soaked clothes off newly tended wounds, was already patchy with spots of blood and ointment.

Bottom line: Cole *was* hurt. And it was because of her. "A boat exploded thirty feet away from us. My ears are still ringing, and I feel as if I was hit by a truck even though there's barely a mark on me. You, on the other hand…" She left the sentence undone. Where could she even begin? He'd played human shield and nearly paid for it with his life. "Stop saying everything's fine." Endless stacks of emotions piled heavily on her heart, demanding to be heard. Tears stung her eyes and her nose burned. "This is not fine!"

She couldn't stop the sharp sob that broke from her lips. The sound came without warning. Rita clamped a hand over her mouth and turned on her heels for the bathroom where she could drown her worries in a hot shower and wash the stink of river water away. "Excuse me," she cried on her way down the hall. "I have to call Mrs. Wilcox and check on my cats."

She reemerged thirty minutes later, fresh out of tears and ways to fix her puffy eyes. Clean, dry and dressed in her favorite white cotton top and pale gray leggings, she felt almost normal. With any luck, she didn't look like the same frantic nut who'd gone into the bathroom half an hour before.

Her mouth watered as she padded down the short hallway toward the kitchen. The house outside the bathroom smelled like heaven.

Cole stood at the stove, shirtless, pushing sliced peppers, onions and mushrooms around a pan. Rice boiled in the pot beside him. He flicked a troubled gaze her way. "How was the shower?"

"Good." She leaned against the counter behind him

in the narrow space, examining the angry red burns and other assorted injuries on his back and shoulders. Beneath today's cuts and burns, a palette of heavy scars rose in permanent welts. Shrapnel. Rita knew those scars well. She'd lived on a dozen army bases growing up, and too many men had similar war wounds. Some had much worse. And they were still the lucky ones because they'd made it home.

Rita had known that Cole was a veteran, but she'd never considered that this wasn't his first run-in with a bomb. "Your uncle gave me everything I need to change your bandages after your shower."

Cole froze for a beat, then went busily back to work at the stove. "Hungry?"

Her tummy rumbled audibly. "Yes."

Cole removed the sauté pan from the stove top and drained the rice before turning to face her for the first time since she'd walked in on him shirtless and cooking. He'd traded his wet socks and uniform pants for bare feet and basketball shorts. The shorts hung dangerously low on his torso, daring her eyes to follow the path of dark hair from his belly button to where it disappeared beneath his waistband.

When she finally found the strength to pry her curious eyes off his body, Cole was staring.

"Everything okay?" he asked through a playful grin.

"Mmm-hmm." She pressed her lips together in embarrassment.

"Good." He inhaled deeply. "How are your cats?"

"Fine. Mrs. Wilcox is meeting all their demands."

Cole grinned. "I made dinner, but I should confess first. There's an ulterior motive behind it."

Rita felt her eyebrows rise to the ceiling.

"I think we should talk about some of the things that happened today," he said.

"Okay."

Cole rubbed the back of his neck, making his chest appear doubly broad. He winced. His arm lowered at a much slower pace than he'd used to raise it. Frustration changed his gentle expression into something resembling the face he'd worn on the docks.

"Why were you angry when you woke in the water?" Rita bit her tongue once the words were out. She hadn't meant to ask so abruptly, but she had to know. She'd upset him somehow and deserved to know what happened.

Cole shifted his weight and let his arms drop to his sides. "I wasn't angry."

"Yes," she argued. "You were. You barely spoke to me the whole time we were on the dock. You snapped at your uncle when he tried to help you. I don't know what I did that made you so mad, but I'm sorry."

Cole crossed his arms and waited. A mask of patience replaced the frustration she'd seen on him earlier.

The more she spoke, the bolder she felt. "Was it because you had to throw me off the boat? Because I panicked and I couldn't move." Cole wasn't arguing his side, interrupting or diminishing her position. He was listening. And she loved it. "I knew I needed to run, but I couldn't."

He reached for her cheek, brushing away another

determined tear. "I wasn't angry with you. I was disappointed in myself. You needed me to protect you, and I failed."

"You were hit with the fiery hull of an exploding boat. It's not like you were home watching the game."

He laughed, and the room seemed brighter. "A blackout is no excuse."

"You saved my life again," she said. "So what if I got to help you out, too?"

"It's my job to protect you. Not the other way around." He turned back to the stove and plated the rice and veggies. "You don't have to take care of everyone all the time. I don't want you looking at me like I'm your little brother. I don't want to be parented."

Anger pinched her chest. "I wasn't parenting you. I kissed you! You think I want to kiss my brother?"

He pushed heaping plates of rice and veggies onto the island beside two glasses of ice water, napkins and silverware. "Eat. You haven't had anything all day, and you're shaking."

Rita moved to a stool at the counter. "Who's the parent now?"

"Not me." He exhaled the words. "I'm the little brother who should've been a doctor."

Rita let the words settle in. "Do you really think that, or are you just repeating the things your brother and uncle said today?"

Cole wiped his hands on a towel and tossed the cloth onto his counter. "I don't regret being a deputy. I was meant to do this, and they know it. I only tried medical school because it made my parents happy. When I left the military, they wanted to see me do something safe, but I'm not a doctor, I'm a lawman." He locked her in his stare. "This is who I am."

"I like who you are," Rita whispered.

Cole made a move in her direction, his smart blue eyes never leaving hers. "I can protect you."

Rita wet her lips. "I know."

A small smile tugged his lips. "Since you're going to be staying here, I think we need some rules."

She forced herself to breathe. His slow, predatory walk was churning her thoughts into mush. "We do?"

"My house. My rules. Ready?"

"Um."

"First, you're my guest. That means I make the meals, shower second and sleep on the couch. You get the bed, hot water and as many of my meals as you can tolerate."

Rita bit her lip against the argument on her tongue. Cole had let her talk when she needed to. It was her turn to listen.

"Second, you're under my protection now, so if something else blows up, it's not going to be you. And if I get knocked out again, don't baby me. Just slap my face and tell me to wake the hell up and get back to work."

Rita laughed. "Fine. Did you really go to Stanford?"

Cole took the seat at her side, stuffing the next closest bar stool beneath him. "For a minute."

"Impressive."

He forked a pile of peppers before lifting a broad and youthful smile to her. "You think so?"

"Yeah."

He stuffed the bite into his mouth and chewed thoughtfully. "You like smart guys. I figured. Suit-and-tie guys with loafers and 401Ks."

"What?" Rita laughed, nearly losing the mouthful of delicious dinner. "No. I mean, not no, but not only suits. I'm a very nondiscriminatory dater. Or I would be if anyone ever asked me out. No one asks."

"What?" Cole dropped his fork onto his plate. His mouth hung open briefly before curving into a disbelieving smile. "No one asks, or you never say yes?"

"Both, I guess, but mostly the first one."

"Why?" he pressed, inexplicably mystified.

"I can be a little distrusting," she admitted, "and I didn't want the distraction while Ryan was living with me. Now that he's on his own, I'm a little older and a lot of folks are married."

"I'm not married."

Rita's smile widened. "Well, Dad warned me about dating soldiers."

Cole grinned. "Yeah?"

"That's what he said, which is silly because he's a general. Though, in hindsight, it probably saved him a lot of trouble considering my high school years were spent on a series of army bases."

"Your dad sounds like a wise man."

"Really? I expected you to disagree."

"Why? Because I was a soldier?" Cole faced her. "I'm actually a huge fan of whatever has kept you single this long."

Rita poked her dinner, unable to eat with so much nervous energy raging inside her. "I think I was waiting for someone special. A man with brains and brawn. A hero's heart. A strong sense of justice and ties to the community."

Cole slid onto his feet, crowding her personal space. "That's a hefty list."

He grabbed her hips and turned her to face him.

Rita's knees parted on instinct, making room for him to get closer.

"Anything else?" Cole widened his stance, bringing him marginally closer to her height.

She craned her neck for a better look at his handsome face. "Yeah."

Heat from his bare chest radiated out to her, and the look in his eyes turned her bones into putty.

She braced her hands on his shoulders, then slid her open palms against his neck, tracing the strong line of his jaw with her thumbs. "My dream guy would know when to kiss me."

Cole's smiling lips were instantly on hers. Soft and testing at first, then heavy and urging.

She wound her fingers into his hair and hooked an ankle behind his leg, nudging him closer. The little gasp that burst from her lips was met with a low, sexy growl.

The day had just gotten a whole lot better.

Until the ringing landline stilled his mouth on hers.

Cole froze, tightening his fingers on her hips as if she might disappear.

"Do you have to get that?" she asked, hoping desperately he'd decide to carry her to his room instead of taking the call. She'd been replaying their earlier kiss since she'd taken one look at him making her dinner.

Shirtless. Could it get any better? Her body responded to his so easily, melding into his touch and matching him, heat for heat, as if this was just one more in a life-time of shared kisses instead of only their second.

He kissed her again, and she parted her lips for him, inviting him deeper. Cole's tongue swept into her mouth, and suddenly, she could think of several ways this could get better.

Cole pulled back by a fraction and stared pointedly into her eyes. "Yes, but don't go anywhere."

Rita fanned her cheeks as Cole went to grab the land-line, still ringing rudely on the wall.

"Garrett." He shifted his gaze back to Rita. "Who's calling?" Color bled from his ruddy cheeks. "One min-ute." Cole returned to her side, phone extended. "It's for you."

Rita pressed the phone to her ear, more terrified by the look on Cole's face than by anything she'd seen or experienced all week. "This is Rita Horn."

Cole grabbed a T-shirt off the back of a nearby chair and tugged it over his head, then scooped keys and a wallet off the table by his front door.

"Miss Horn," the stranger's voice began, "this is Mercy Medical Center. Your brother, Ryan Horn, has been in a serious car accident."

Chapter Twelve

Rita jammed bare feet into untied running shoes. *Ryan was hurt.* A car accident. He was at the hospital, and she needed to go.

Emergency Room doors...west wing...second floor.

Cole had her purse and jacket over one arm. "Ready?"

"Thank you." She slid shaking arms into the sleeves of her hoodie and zipped it to her chin. A round of powerful tremors rattled her teeth and twisted her stomach. She'd forgotten about the truck. She'd forgotten about her own brother. She was a horrible sister. A terrible substitute parent. *Mom would have never forgotten him.*

Cole opened the front door and held it for Rita to pass.

A moment later, they were on their way to the hospital at unlawful speeds. The cruiser's lights and sirens cleared a path as they moved through the compact downtown streets.

Rita wound noodle arms around her middle, certain that losing Ryan would tear her in two. "The last communication I had with him was through text messages, and I argued with him about my truck. I never argue with him. Why would I do that?"

Cole moved an open palm onto her thigh. "You were trying to keep him safe."

"Yeah," she scoffed, "by lying to him. I promised to always be honest. Always be truthful, but I've been lying to Ryan since the minute I got involved in this mess with Minsk. I broke my promise."

Cole's thumb swept across her skin in soothing waves. "This isn't your fault. It was an accident. And he's going to be okay."

Rita curled her fingers over his and pulled their joined hands to her cheek. This wasn't the first time she'd rushed to the hospital after someone she loved had been in a car accident. "How do you know?"

"He's your brother, right? I bet he's tough."

"He is."

Cole offered her an encouraging smile. "He'll pull through this, and while he's doing that, I'll be with you every step of the way."

The last time she'd been in this situation, things hadn't been okay. Not ever again. "My mom didn't pull through."

Cole gave her a long look. "Do you want to talk about it?"

No, she didn't want to, but the words were already filling her mouth. The fear constricting her chest. "The man who hit my mother was in for his eleventh DUI when he was released due to overcrowding in the jails. A lot of low-level offenders were set free. I guess that was what he was until he killed my mother. Not that he was charged with her death. Wasn't the first time he'd been incarcerated for driving under the influence or the first time he'd been released without a license, only to get behind the wheel again. Drunk."

Cole's strong expression crumbled. Heartbreak swam in his eyes. "I'm so sorry."

"He didn't actually hit her," Rita blabbed on. "Nothing like that. He was just going the wrong way on the highway at night. My mom swerved, attempting not to die in a head-on collision. Ironic, right? The only life she saved was the drunk's. He got off with a slap on the wrist and a stern talking-to. His lawyer argued that he didn't hit her. She'd acted on her own. He said maybe she saw a deer or something. That was the defense's argument. How could we prove that she'd swerved to miss the drunk driver? He got another DUI, a frowny face for driving without a license and some nonsense about not obeying traffic signs. He's probably out there now, doing it again."

"Rita." Cole's voice was husky and thick with regret.

The hospital came into view, tall and regal on the horizon. A giant red cross stretched from the roof with the word Mercy emblazoned in white across its middle.

"I'm fine." Rita released Cole's hand in favor of unbuckling her seat belt and wiping her face. The tears had dried as suddenly as they'd come. "The hospital said Ryan swerved."

Cole left his cruiser in valet parking, but took the key and darted around to meet Rita.

She was already making strides toward the sliding glass doors.

"Where are we going?" Cole asked, taking her hand once more.

"He's in surgery." She racked her brain to remember the voice from the phone. "Second floor, I think."

"I know that one. That's the trauma unit. Come on." He pulled her into a jog, bypassing the giant silver elevator in favor of a doorway marked Stairs.

The second floor waiting room was vast but silent. Bitter scents of burned coffee and popcorn hung in the air, creeping in from the main hall. A sleeping woman tipped awkwardly in one chair, having apparently fallen asleep while knitting, needles still in her hands, yarn on her lap.

Cole kept moving until they reached the nurses' station. "This is Rita Horn. I'm Deputy Cole Garrett. We received a call that her brother, Ryan Horn, was in a car accident. He's in surgery now."

The woman slid a clipboard onto the counter. Her chair knocked against the table, spilling an open bag of microwave popcorn over her workstation. Rita's stomach knotted at the sight of it. "Miss Horn, you were listed as Ryan's next of kin. Is there anyone else you'd like us to notify for you?"

"No. I'll take care of that."

"I don't mind," the woman pressed. "I know this is hard."

Rita shot her a disbelieving look. Did she know? How could she? When was the last time she'd gotten a call like this about her baby brother? Rita bit her tongue against the building tirade. "Our dad's overseas. I don't even know where, exactly." Government secrets and all. She fought an internal eyeroll. Once again she was on her own to deal with a family crisis while the supposed head of the household was off to who-knew-where. "He has a number and an email address that he checks when he can. I'll handle it." She took the clipboard. "What's this?"

"We'll need your brother's complete medical history, insurance and contact information. Also, your brother is an organ donor. If you have any questions about that, I'm prepared to answer them."

Rita hugged the clipboard to her chest. "I'm well informed on that matter. Thank you. What I need to know is how my brother is doing." Tears began to fall once more, ruining her attempt to look strong when Ryan needed her.

"I won't know any more than you do until he's out of surgery."

Rita whipped the clipboard in the air, desperate to smack something with it, and knowing she just looked crazy. A rough sob ripped through her.

The nurse's expression turned solemn. "I'm sorry."

Cole dragged Rita against him, wrapping strong arms around her back and cradling her head to his chest. "Can you tell us anything about what happened?" he asked the woman behind the desk.

"No. Only that he was involved in a car accident. Maybe someone at the sheriff's department will have more details."

"Thank you. You'll let us know as soon as he's out of surgery?"

"A doctor will find you."

Cole led Rita to an exterior terrace on the opposite end of the floor. "I need to make some calls. It's private here."

Rita took a seat, unsure if her legs would hold her up much longer. Beyond the glass, a cafeteria with neon lights promised *Good Food! Cold Drinks!*

Cole worked a phone from the pocket of his shorts and flipped it open. "Burner," he explained. "I lose more phones than you'd think. I have a few of these for emergencies." He pressed the buttons on a tiny keypad, then caught the phone between his ear and shoulder.

Three calls and ten minutes later, Cole lowered into a squat before her. "Lomar was the deputy on scene at Ryan's accident. He said Uncle Henry was the first responder. That's very good news. Henry's the best. I've put a call in to him, too."

Rita lifted her eyes to Cole's, buoyed by the small measure of hope. "Did you talk to Lomar?"

"Yes."

"Was Ryan driving my truck?" She braced herself for the answer she feared was coming.

"Yes."

A rush of breath swept from her lungs. This was the very thing she'd feared most. Ryan had taken her truck, then someone had mistaken him for her and tried to kill him. She didn't need to hear the details to know that was the truth of it. Ryan was a careful driver, and her truck was in sound condition. An accident today, after the day she'd had seemed highly unlikely.

Ryan was in critical condition and it was her fault. "Was he alone?" she asked, realizing the roommate he was helping move might've somehow gotten wrapped up in her mess, too. What if the other kid hadn't been as lucky as Ryan? Ryan had at least made it into surgery.

That was more than her Mom had.

"He was alone," Cole said. "I have some limited details now. They're yours if you want them, but if you want to wait until you know Ryan's out of surgery, there's no rush."

Images of Ryan's crash, or her mind's version of it anyway, raced through her head. He had to be okay. She couldn't live in a world where her determination to help an injured kitten had caused her brother's eventual death.

"I want to know." She pressed her palms against her knees. "I want to know everything you know. Please."

Cole nodded. "Okay. First, why don't you call your dad?" He tipped his phone in her direction. "Then we can move to the waiting area and watch for the doctor to come out of surgery."

COLE FOLLOWED RITA to a pair of chairs near the window. The call to her father had been short and sweet. A message on a voice mail. There was nothing else she could do.

"Okay," she said. "Tell me what you know."

"Deputy Lomar was the responding officer," he began. "Dispatch pulled him from the marina after a witness called to report the accident."

"There was a witness?" Hope lit her beautiful face.

"Yes. A jogger says she saw your truck moving at

questionable speeds on the county route between the college and Crestmont Hills in Rivertown."

"That's Ryan's neighborhood."

"The jogger said the truck was speeding and heading into a dangerous curve. She assumed he wasn't paying attention, or maybe he'd been drinking, but when Ryan passed her, she got a look at his face. She described him as terrified. Stiff armed. The truck was loaded with furniture, the hill he was headed down was steep, and she was right, he didn't make the curve at the bottom. He lost control and hit a tree. Based on the damage to your truck, Lomar estimates Ryan attempted a twenty-mile-per-hour curve at more than fifty. Also, there weren't any tire marks on the pavement."

"He didn't use the brakes?" Rita pressed the heels of her hands against red eyes. "I don't suppose the jogger happened to notice an evil psychopath in a black sedan nearby."

"No. There were no other cars at the time of the accident. I think we should count that as a blessing," Cole said. "No one could have maneuvered the truck around traffic at those speeds."

"Right." Rita raked her hands through her hair and gripped the back of her head. "So we can assume someone cut the brakes. Obviously, this was the same person who's been trying to kill me all day, and now they've nearly killed Ryan, instead."

"We don't know anything for certain," Cole cautioned. "Lomar's looking into it now. He'll be here when he finishes."

Rita clenched her jaw. "I just had the truck serviced,

and it was fine when I drove it home before Ryan borrowed it. The only way there wouldn't be any tire marks from this accident is if the brakes didn't engage."

Cole leaned closer, lowering his voice as he spoke. "*If* someone cut the brake lines, and trust me, I'm not trying to create a conspiracy theory here, but if that's what happened, given the day we've had, I would agree. It's fair to assume this wasn't a coincidence."

Rita nodded. Good. He was still on her side.

"And if someone wanted to cause an accident," he continued, "they would make sure the damage to the brake line was small and the leak was slow. Someone who knew what they were doing would want brake fluid in the lines when the driver got in, maybe even enough to last while Ryan confidently collected furniture for a new roommate before running out. If he got into the truck and there were no brakes, he wouldn't have gone anywhere, except maybe to a garage, and that would've ruined the criminal's efforts. Wasted his time."

Rita slumped forward. "By the time Ryan was on the county route, loaded down and driving faster, using the brakes for hills and turns, the fluid would've run out, and it would've been too late to stop."

"That's what I'm thinking," Cole admitted. "You know about cars?"

"Just brakes. My first car had soft brakes, and Dad was home at the time. He found the problem and told me what could happen if I'd kept driving it that way. Said I wasted my money on a junker car when I could've walked anywhere I needed to go."

Criticizing his only daughter? Telling her to walk

after learning she'd saved for a car? What a jerk. Cole forced a tight smile. "Your dad sounds like a real peach."

"Yep."

Clearly, Rita had gotten her kind and nurturing heart from her mother.

Two long hours later, a man in blue scrubs stopped at the nurses' station outside the waiting room, then turned to face Cole and Rita when the nurse pointed their way.

Rita leaped from her chair and met the man in the hallway. Cole followed.

According to the man's name tag he was chief of surgery.

"I'm Dr. Keller." He hugged his clipboard in one arm and extended his free hand to Rita, then Cole. "Ryan's surgery was textbook. No complications. No surprises. He's being moved from Recovery to an observation room on this floor now."

Rita lifted onto her toes, craning her neck to see around the doctor. "Which room is his? Can I talk to him now?"

"You're welcome to see him, but talking to him will take some time."

Her jaw dropped. "Why?"

Cole pulled her against his side and curved a protective arm around her waist. He'd seen what she hadn't yet. The tight set of the doctor's jaw. His rigid stance. The slight pinch of his mouth, indicating that he'd delivered the only good news he had.

Dr. Keller shuffled his bootie-covered feet. "Your brother has been unconscious since his arrival. You're more than welcome to talk to him, but he's unlikely to respond. Though I like to think all communication helps, one-sided or not."

Rita crunched her brow. "I don't understand. When will he wake up?"

The doctor shifted his gaze to Cole.

"It's okay," Cole answered the unspoken question. "She can handle it."

Dr. Keller lowered his chin before turning back to Rita. "As you may have been told, Ryan's injuries are extensive. He has multiple fractures to his hands, arms and ribs, plus his right foot and left thigh. There's significant damage to the bones in his cheek, forehead and upper jaw. He'll need additional surgeries to correct those issues later. I was able to locate and stop his internal bleeding, and set several broken bones. It was a good start. Right now, we're concerned about secondary injuries that often occur in situations like these. Sometimes it takes a day or two after a trauma for things to rear their heads. We're watching specifically for signs of swelling or bruising of the brain. The anesthesia should've worn off in Recovery. Now, it's just a matter of when he opens his eyes. We'll know more once he wakes. Any other questions?"

Rita gaped.

Cole hugged her tight. "We want to see him."

"Of course." Dr. Keller led the way to a private room near the nurses' station. "Visiting hours are shorter here than the other wards. The patients need extended time to rest. Also, we ask that they have no more than one visitor at a time. I'm sure you understand."

"No." Rita stopped short. "Two." She faced off with the doctor. "Two at a time, and I'm not leaving until he wakes up. I don't care about your hours. I won't make a sound, and I'll stay out of the way, but I won't leave him."

Dr. Keller made an apologetic face. "Hospital policy says…"

"Sir," Cole interrupted before the man could tell her no. He dragged his badge from one pocket and flipped it open, well aware that he looked absolutely nothing like a lawman in his running shorts and faded army T-shirt. "I'm a deputy with the Cade County Sheriff's Department, and we have reason to believe this young man's vehicle was tampered with. For his safety, we'll need a deputy stationed outside the door at all times, and I'll be staying with Miss Horn. She and her brother are going through a terrible ordeal right now, and all they have is each other."

The words were sour on his tongue. Rita had Cole, too, and he needed to tell her. She deserved to know the things that had been happening to his heart since their lives crossed paths this week. He'd never felt so attached to or identified so strongly with anyone who wasn't blood related. Hell, he'd never even met Ryan, but the guy lying in that bed may as well have been his brother. At least, that was the way it seemed to his heart as it pounded and his breaths grew shallow. He needed that young man to be okay because Rita needed him to be okay.

"Fine." Dr. Keller didn't look pleased, but he also didn't argue. "Get a chair for the other deputy from the waiting area. You can place it in the hallway outside his door. The security detail is required to stay outside the room, and he can't bother the nurses. They have work to do. I'll allow you to accompany Miss Horn inside the room on a probational basis, but only you."

"Yes, sir."

RITA UNTANGLED HERSELF from Cole's grasp and darted to Ryan's side on autopilot. She dragged her fingers over the cold metal railing, drinking in the sting of antiseptic in the air.

The man in the bed looked nothing like her baby brother, and yet he was exactly that. His face was purple and deeply bruised, swollen to the extreme and distorted by the injuries. His head was wrapped in gauze. Tubes ran from freestanding machines into the crook of his arm and up his nose. Rita recalled the sweet scent of oxygen through her mask at the river and hoped Ryan was as relieved by the clean air as she had been.

She lifted his bandaged fingers in hers. A cast ran the length of his arm to his palm. "Ry?" She stroked the backs of his fingertips with her thumb. "I am so sorry," she whispered, drying tears as they fell. "This is all my fault, and if you can hear me, you've got to wake up so I can make it right. I owe you a huge explanation, then you can yell at me and tell me how stupid I am." She jiggled his motionless hand in hers. "Wake up and tell me I'm stupid."

Wake up so I know I didn't get you killed.

COLE MOVED TO stand behind Rita. He rubbed her shoulders. He checked the time on a large clock outside the door. The county municipal building would close in half an hour, and no one had been down there to ask what Minsk was doing during his recent visits. Cole wanted to be the one to get those answers.

Rita pressed one palm to her brother's misshapen face. He looked like Frankenstein's monster now, but the swelling would go away soon, and a plastic surgeon would return him to the image Rita remembered. Cole had seen a lot worse injuries heal to near invisibility.

"Hey." He leaned his mouth to her ear. "Any chance I can convince you to make a trip to the courthouse?"

"No."

"Okay." He'd figured.

The minute hand on the clock took another step toward closing time at the courthouse, but there was no way Cole would leave Rita alone again, not even at a hospital. Not even with another deputy as her personal guardian. Protecting her was Cole's job now, and he didn't trust anyone else to get it done.

"I can't leave him." She turned to Cole, burying her face in the contours of his chest. "What if he wakes up and I'm not here? What if he doesn't wake up?" Her chest thumped and rattled with shuttered breaths. "I can't."

Cole stroked the length of her soft red hair. "Okay. We'll stay." Maybe he could sneak into the hall later and make some calls from the nurse's desk.

Rita stroked his chest with one hand. She rolled her head to press a cheek against his tear-soaked shirt. "Do you think there's a chance that this is all just horrible timing? Maybe I assumed the worse, and this was just an accident and it isn't my fault."

Cole pressed a kiss to the top of her head. He gripped her tight around the middle and wished he could give her hope. But he didn't believe in coincidence, and this catastrophe was too spot-on to be anything other than intentional.

"Deputy Garrett?" Deputy Lomar's voice turned Cole's head toward the open door.

Rita tightened her arms around Cole's waist and angled her face away from the deputy.

Cole adjusted his hold on instinct, careful to keep her secure and comforted, even in the presence of another deputy. Especially one who'd been his wingman at more than one bar this month. The only other single man on the job should know Rita Horn wasn't up for grabs. She was Cole's, and he'd be hers in a minute if she wanted him. "Any news?"

Lomar's gaze lingered on Cole's hands, placed low and protectively on Rita's trim body. Lomar knew Cole didn't do PDA. He didn't get involved beyond a bar and a beer. Until now, a *long-term relationship* had meant sharing a bed until dawn. Cole had never made a secret of his intentional bachelorhood. The whole department knew it. Hell, half the town knew it, and by the way Lomar was staring, the whole of Cade County would know about the drastic change in him by dinner.

"You have an update?" Cole prompted, lifting his chin in defiance.

Lomar cleared his throat. "Yeah." His curious eyes

jumped back to meet Cole's. "Cade County Automotive was able to confirm the cause of the accident."

"And?"

"Someone cut the truck's brake lines."

Chapter Thirteen

Rita fell asleep at Ryan's bedside to the soft, repetitive beeping and whooshing of hospital equipment. When her eyes opened again, the room was dark. Tiny red and green lights illuminated the corner, occasionally backlit by small screens, assuring her the machines attached to her brother were still doing all they could to monitor him. Her head rested on the edge of his bed, her bottom on the rough cushion of a wooden hospital chair.

She brushed her fingers gently against his bruised cheek. "Come on, Ry. Time to wake up."

Cole shifted in his sleep. His long body was spread over the awful green recliner in the room's corner, limbs dangling, head cocked awkwardly. He'd chosen a seat with full view of the hallway outside, then set up a makeshift office utilizing a Wi-Fi password schmoozed off the nurse and the laptop he'd pulled from his cruiser. He should have gone home for some proper rest, but she was selfishly thankful he hadn't. She'd wanted him there. More than that, she'd wanted him to *want* to stay.

And he had.

Rita's tummy growled and she pressed a palm against

her middle to stifle the noise. The green Jell-O and cup of ice chips Cole had delivered around midnight had worn off long ago. She'd been too upset to consider eating anything more substantial at the time, but currently, she'd like a tall stack of hotcakes with a double side of bacon.

Her head ached with every move she made. Her neck was stiff from the awkward position she'd temporarily slept in. She scooped the plastic cup of melted ice chips off the nightstand and sucked down the few measly teaspoons of liquid. She'd cheerfully have gone in search of more, if it hadn't meant leaving Ryan.

The room's door swung open, and a young woman swept back the privacy curtain separating them from the nurses' station on the other side of the observation glass.

Cole had pulled the curtain before Rita fell asleep.

The nurse started. "Oh, hello." She brushed wild brown curls away from her face. Her cheeks darkened, and she darted her attention from Rita to Ryan and back. "I didn't know you were awake. I'm Stacy." She hung a pink stethoscope around her neck. "I'm the night nurse. How are you holding up?"

Rita bobbed her head and forced a tight smile. "Awful."

"Yeah. I figured." Stacy moved to Ryan's side. "It's hard to see our loved ones like this. Most folks stay in the waiting room, if they stay at all." She checked the tubes running to and from him, then tapped the IV bag. "Good." She pulled a small pad of paper from her pocket and made a note, then checked the machines. "Everything looks really great." She turned back to Rita with a warm smile and raised brows. "Your brother's tough. He'll get through this. He talks about you a lot, you know?"

"You know Ryan?" Rita jerked upright, greedy for information. Her pounding head nearly knocked her out. "Ow." She rubbed her temple and cringed.

Stacy moved to Rita's side. "May I?" She caught Rita's wrist in her small fingers without waiting for an answer. "Your pulse is racing. The other nurses said you've barely eaten since you got here yesterday afternoon, and those ice chips don't make much water."

Rita already knew that. She wanted the information she didn't have. "How do you know Ryan?"

"School." Stacy leaned her backside against the bed and gripped the railing on each side of her. "I'm an RN, but I'm going to be a nurse practitioner next year. I take classes during the day, and I see him around sometimes." She lifted her gaze to Rita's forehead where the goose bump looked like the beginnings of a second head.

"Is he happy?" Rita asked.

"Yeah. Always smiling. Funny. Kind."

Fresh tears welled in Rita's eyes. "Thank you for saying that."

"It's no problem. He's a great guy." Stacy stuffed her hands into her pockets. "I hate that this happened to him."

"Me, too."

Stacy stroked the length of Ryan's arm cast. "He's going to be okay. It looks scary now, but this will all heal." She glanced through the window wall, then turned her back to it. "His leg had the most damage. The femur was shattered, but it's not a life-or-death injury, and his brain and spinal column look good."

Rita covered her mouth, outrageously thankful for the details. "Dr. Keller made me think Ryan might not wake up."

"He'll wake up," Stacy assured her. "I know it." She gave him a lingering look. "A career in professional basketball or the military might be out, but he'll be okay."

Stacy smiled at her joke, but Rita ached internally. Ryan had wanted a career in the military and she'd inadvertently taken that from him by allowing this accident.

Stacy finished up and left without a goodbye.

She returned a few minutes later with food. "It's Marcia's birthday today, so we have one of those giant sub sandwiches in the break room. I thought you might like a piece."

Salty scents of ham and cheese wafted out to meet her. Rich, buttery Italian bread. The tangy bite of onions and pickles. "Thank you." Rita accepted the plate with a greedy smile.

"But wait. There's more." Stacy dropped a bottle of water onto the table beside Rita's empty cup. "And…" She dug in her pocket and came out with a two-pack of aspirin. "For your headache."

"How do you know I have a headache?"

Stacy shook her head. "You're squinting and rubbing your temple. You haven't eaten and you're under a ton of stress. If you didn't need some kind of pill at this point, I'd wonder if you were human."

"Bless you." Rita tossed the two aspirin onto her

tongue and washed them down with half the bottle of water.

"Don't mention it. I'll be back to check on you after you've had time to eat." She squeezed Ryan's blanket-covered foot on her way out.

Rita really needed to ask him about this woman when he woke up.

She finished the water and sandwich in minutes.

The door opened again, and Stacy reappeared with a folded manila envelope. "How was dinner?" Her attention lingered on Ryan's quiet form.

Rita dusted her palms. "Excellent. Thank you." Behind her, Cole shifted in the too-small chair. He deserved a thank-you for staying with her when he wanted to be out working the case. She didn't like that she'd kept him from it, but she was glad he'd fallen asleep. He needed rest to heal.

Cole yawned. "What time is it?"

Stacy checked her watch. "Four fifteen."

"This is Stacy," Rita explained by way of introduction. "She's Ryan's night nurse and knows him from school."

"Small world," Cole said, sliding to the edge of his seat and extending a hand to Stacy.

"Small town," Stacy added.

"I'm Cole Garrett," he said, "nice to meet you."

She smiled. "Yes, I've seen you around, Deputy Garrett. I'm glad you're here." She turned her attention back to Rita. "I thought you might want this." She extended the envelope in Rita's direction. "This was at the nurses' station. I assume it's everything Ryan had on him when they took him in for surgery. You should keep it until he wakes up." She gave a soft smile. "I'd better get to work. I'll bring another water when I come back. Can I get you anything, Deputy Garrett?"

"Coffee?"

"Sure thing." Stacy slipped back through the door, leaving it ajar.

Cole tracked her movement through the window before turning narrowed eyes on Rita. "Nurses are usually nice to me, but I've never had one taking drink orders."

"I think she's got something going with my brother." Rita turned the envelope over in her hands, examining it top to bottom. Was it nosy of her to want to look?

"Did she say that?" Cole stretched to his feet, brows puckered. He rolled his shoulders and swore softly.

"You're hurt. It's way past time to change your bandages." Rita sighed. She was normally good in a crisis, but lately there had been just too many emergencies to keep tabs on. "She didn't say it, but I can tell."

"How?"

Rita made a face. "Well, don't look so mystified. You can tell when women are into you. Same thing here."

Cole snorted. "I can tell because they say so."

Rita rubbed her eyes to stop them from rolling. She considered judging the women who'd been bold enough to tell Cole Garrett they wanted him, but hadn't she climbed onto his lap yesterday and basically assaulted him?

She let her eyes fall shut. She was jealous of faceless, unnamed women who may or may not have behaved exactly like she had.

"Rita?" Cole nudged her elbow. "You okay?"

"I'm super." She opened her eyes, then flipped the envelope over on her legs and slid a tentative finger beneath the partially glued flap. Either someone had done a terrible job of sealing it, or someone had taken a peek inside. She lifted her eyes to the window wall, locating Stacy in the hallway with ease. Would she have pried into Ryan's personal things?

"Was that already open?" Cole asked.

"I'm not sure." Rita upturned the envelope and shook the contents onto her lap. A wallet. Phone. Loose change. Keys. Nothing unusual.

Cole leaned in. "Anything missing that you think ought to be there?"

"I don't know what he normally carries with him." She opened his wallet and checked for cash. Thirty-two dollars. "He had money." Emotion tightened her chest. "I'm always afraid he won't have enough cash to eat or buy gas or do the things he wants to do." She flipped through the pictures. One of their parents. One of Rita. None of Stacy the potential girlfriend or very nosy nurse. "I'm glad he had some money." There was something else inside she couldn't see. The raised area was among his credit card slots, but sheltered by a small leather flap. She wiggled her fingernail inside and extracted the contents. "Oh, my gosh, he has a condom."

Cole laughed.

She pushed everything back inside the leather bifold and shook her hands out at the wrists. "I didn't even know he was dating. Oh. Ugh. What if he isn't dating?"

What if he was a player? A no-commitment type? She bit her lip. *That would make him just like Cole.*

All sex. No strings.

She ignored the ice block sliding through her gut. "Why doesn't he talk to me about this stuff?"

Cole scoffed. "Why would he?"

"Because we're friends, and aren't siblings supposed to talk about things?" She looked to Cole for input. This was clearly more his territory than hers.

Cole rubbed his chin. "I don't know. I've got three older brothers, and we don't talk about sex. Surely you knew he was having sex."

"Stop saying that."

"What? Sex?"

Rita pointed a warning finger at him. "Stop."

His expression rode the line between confusion and amusement. "He's in college. What do you think happens in a town with twenty-thousand single people of age?"

"He's supposed to be in college to learn," she said. "I didn't need condoms when I was in college." She regretted the choice of words immediately.

It was too much information, and it was out there now.

Cole cocked his head. "Never? What exactly are you saying?" A twist of shock and intrigue edged his words. He'd somehow picked up on the thing she hadn't said. An implication that was barely made.

Rita wet her lips, then pressed them tight.

"I mean, it's none of my business, but…" He moved into her space and dropped into a squat before her.

"Rita?" His probing blue eyes examined her with intensity, having easily and accurately jumped to the borderline embarrassing conclusion. "When was the last time you needed a condom?"

She lowered her gaze. Truth be told, Rita hadn't even seen a condom in years. Her one and only serious boyfriend, a fellow senior from her high school *du jour*, had purchased the only package of protection she'd thought she had use for, but thanks to his cheating ways, the grand finale of a goodbye she'd had planned was ruined. Rita's virginity had stayed intact. Much as she'd wanted that guy to be her first, there was no room for sharing in her heart. She wouldn't give herself over to someone who didn't regard her highly enough to be exclusive with their intimacy. Not then, and not now. After that, she left for college. Then her mom died, and Ryan became her priority. Work took second place, and everything else was irrelevant.

"Rita?"

She shook her head. She'd idealized sex for years because it had meant so much to her as a high schooler, but suddenly the notion of saving herself for true love seemed juvenile and dumb.

Rita grabbed the envelope hastily and crammed the keys and change inside. "Never," she admitted. There. She'd said it. No sense in lying. Why should it matter?

Before she could get Ryan's wallet back into the envelope, it fell onto the floor, knocked aside by her bumbling hands. The contents scattered, including a folded scrap of white paper she hadn't noticed before.

Cole collected the things in one big mitt and dropped

them into the envelope. "Sorry. I didn't mean to pry. I shouldn't have pushed."

Rita took the envelope and reached inside. "It's fine. What does the paper say?"

She refused to discuss her sex life in front of Ryan, even if he was unconscious.

Maybe Cole had a point about siblings not sharing everything.

She retrieved the neatly folded paper and read the line of uniform text. Her hands began to tremble as she passed the note to Cole.

LEAVE THE PEN UNDER THE MAILBOX AT MEMORIAL PARK. DO IT TONIGHT. COME ALONE. OR YOU'RE NEXT.

Chapter Fourteen

Rage tightened Cole's limbs.

"Stay here." He snatched the scrap of paper from Rita's fingers and went in search of answers. Like how the hell had someone gotten a threatening note into a crash victim's wallet?

Outside Ryan's room, a trio of women in pastel scrubs started. They stared as he held the door wide. He felt his grimace deepen as Lomar's empty chair registered. With Cole inside and Lomar outside, no one should have been able to get anywhere near Rita or her brother. But Cole had fallen asleep and Lomar had apparently taken a walk!

Stacy, the night nurse and note's deliverer, jogged to Cole's side. "What's wrong? Is Ryan okay?" She craned her neck to see into the room behind him, but Cole held his ground.

"Where's Deputy Lomar?"

Stacy looked pointedly at the empty chair. "I don't know. He was there a minute ago. I think."

"You think?"

Stacy swept her anxious gaze back to Cole. "Tell me what happened."

Cole freed the cell phone from his pocket and dialed Lomar. He returned his attention to Stacy as the call connected. "Who delivered the envelope you just brought to Rita?"

The other nurses took a few timid steps in their direction, stopping on Cole's side of their workstation beside an abandoned janitor's bucket. "I believe those were his personal effects," the nurse in blue answered.

"Yes. Who brought them?" he repeated the question through gritted teeth.

The nurses looked at one another.

Cole felt his blood pressure rise. "Where was the envelope?"

Stacy lifted a finger to indicate the opposite side of their curved workstation.

Cole charged in that general direction with Stacy at his heels. "Who could have put it there?"

"I don't know."

"Who has access to this area?" he growled, trying hard not to wake the entire floor with the rush of frustration tearing at his mind.

"Garrett?" Lomar's voice echoed through the phone line and along the quiet corridor to his right.

"Where are you?"

"Here." A set of steady footfalls registered behind Cole and he turned. Lomar putted in his direction, arms bent forward at the elbows, a steaming cup in one hand, giant cookie in the other. He stopped short. "What happened?"

Cole headed for his friend. "Where were you?"

Lomar raised his brows. "Coffee."

"You're not supposed to leave," Cole growled. "You're the protective detail."

Lomar scanned the area, presumably checking each nurse's face for an explanation. "You were inside the room."

"I was asleep!"

"I wasn't gone for two minutes," Lomar barked back. "I walked to the waiting room to pour a cup of coffee, a lady knitting socks gave me a cookie and you called. That's what happened to me. What the hell happened to you?"

What happened to him? Well, someone had taken the time to type up a threat and place it in Ryan's things, either at the accident scene, somehow, or in the ambulance, the operating room... Cole's mind was cluttered with the number of people who could have done this, not to mention the outsiders he hadn't thought of yet, before the note was delivered to Rita. That was what had happened to Cole.

Stacy returned to his side and pointed to an empty shelf near the printer. "I found the envelope here when my shift started, but you and Rita were asleep. I brought it to her as soon as I knew she was up. It probably came from someone in your office. Someone from the crime scene or maybe the operating room. Why?"

Cole turned on her, pinning her with a warning look. "There was a threat in the envelope with Ryan Horn's things. I need to know who had access to this area."

Stacy fell back a step, finally at a loss for words.

"Us," one of the nurses answered. "We're the only

ones on duty from ten until six. Sometimes we see a doctor, but you wouldn't catch a doctor making deliveries."

Then who?

Cole's mind raced. Trauma was a closed ward with a small window of visiting hours and a small number of people who had access. Someone wanted the thumb drive badly enough to take a huge risk delivering that note. Could it be one of the women looking at him now? His eyes roamed back to Lomar's empty chair. Could it be his fellow deputy? Someone present at the accident scene? His fingers curled over the paper, and he forced his mind to work faster.

"Hey," Rita's soft voice sliced through Cole's anger. She leaned in the open doorway of her brother's room, eyes heavy with tears. "How's it going?"

Cole turned away, unwilling to make her night worse with his lack of information and fully ready to lose his mind.

The abandoned mop and bucket stared back at him. He scanned the area for other signs of a cleaning crew. The floors were dry. The ward was silent. Cole marched to the yellow bucket and peered inside. "Where's the janitor?" He turned wild eyes on the nurses. There was no water in the tub. "Whose bucket is this?"

The ladies looked at one another.

Stacy pinched her lip between a thumb and forefinger, apparently in thought.

"What is it?" Cole asked. "Did you see someone cleaning?"

"I saw a man in a janitor's uniform when I made my rounds, but I didn't pay much attention."

"When was that?"

"Not long ago. Only a few minutes before you came out here."

Adrenaline spike in Cole's system, erasing the dull throb of yesterday's burns and igniting his clarity. "What did he look like?" Cole asked.

Stacy shook her head. "I don't know."

Lomar deposited his snacks on the nurses' station and turned to Cole. "He could still be in the building. You want me to make a sweep of the ward. Maybe the floor?"

"No." Cole turned in a small circle, head tipped back. From where he stood, there were at least three cameras in sight. Cole had a better idea. "Where can I review the footage from these cameras?" There was no way anyone got behind that desk without the cameras knowing.

"Tech Support," Stacy said. "Fourth floor. There's a wing of offices and conference rooms. It's in with Security."

"Got it." Cole pressed the note against Lomar's chest. "Bag that and don't let anything happen to her. I'm going to find this guy."

Rita bobbed on her toes, white-knuckle fingers wrapped around the doorjamb. "Don't leave," she pleaded.

Cole's heart ached at the request. Her fearful expression twisted him inside. Fear for herself, for Ryan, for every patient in the building and probably for Cole. Just one more reason he was falling hard and fast for the selfless red-haired beauty. Rita cared for everyone.

He crossed the space to Rita in long, purposeful

strides and planted a kiss on her forehead, hoping the simple touch could convey the things he wasn't yet able to say. "Go back inside and shut the door. Stay with Ryan. Lomar will be right here if you need anything. I'll be back as soon as I can. I won't leave the building without you."

She nodded uneasily, then vanished back into the room and tugged the curtain until only a sliver of her remained visible.

Cole nodded his approval. He hated to leave her, but whoever had followed her this far had chosen to threaten instead of act this time. It seemed to him that that meant recovering the pen she'd found at the docks had taken priority over silencing the witness. She could only tell a jury what she'd seen that night, which wasn't much, but the pen must've had information that someone couldn't afford to have come to light. Whoever wanted it must've thought they'd never get it if they killed her. They didn't know West had already taken that pen for processing.

Cole waved Lomar aside. "Make sure West knows what's going on. We could use some extra boots on the ground if we have them, especially an external patrol of the parking lots and building. If I can't get my hands on this guy before he leaves, we might still be able to catch him making his getaway."

"On it." Lomar dialed Dispatch without missing a beat.

Cole took the stairs to the fourth floor at a run, wincing when the impacts tore at his day-old wounds. He knocked on the security office door with purpose. "Cade County Sheriff's Department. Open up." He held his badge to the glass when a face appeared at the little window.

"Can I help you?" A cheery young woman opened the door and waved him inside.

"I'm Deputy Cole Garrett. I need to see the footage from the second floor trauma ward. Elevator and stairway entries, as well as the nurses' station, over the last thirty minutes."

The girl blinked. "Something wrong?"

Cole could think of at least twenty ways everything was absolutely wrong. "Yes, and we're in a hurry so…"

"Oh." She scrambled onto a rolling chair and swiped her computer to life. "I'm Katie, by the way." Her corkscrew ponytail bobbed and swung as she worked, looking screen to screen on the multi-monitor setup. "Here."

Grainy images of the trauma ward appeared on four screens. On the left, Lomar stood guard outside Ryan's door, keeping careful watch, his eyes on a steady circuit through the space around him. Besides that, the nurses gathered behind their desk. The final two shots showed a still hallway with closed doors for the elevator and stairwell.

"Can you split the screen?" Cole asked. "Cover those four shots at once? Maybe fast forward until we see a janitor." He couldn't afford to miss anything. Rita's life could depend on it.

"Sure." A few more keystrokes and Cole's requests were granted.

He locked and popped his jaw while he waited, looming over the young woman as he searched.

Lomar's head dropped forward, and he jumped to his

feet. He rubbed his eyes, yawned and lifted the disposable cup from its place on the floor by his feet.

Cole fought a twinge of guilt at his anger toward Lomar. He'd been on duty as much as Cole since Minsk had turned up in the river. With a small department like theirs, everyone was overworked when tragedies occurred. This many in a row had to be a record.

Lomar arched his back in the top corner of the screen. He said something, and a nurse pointed down the hall. Lomar checked his watch before hustling away, carrying his cup at comic speed as the time-elapsed feed rolled frantically ahead.

"Him?" Katie lifted a finger to the bottom right corner of her screen. Dressed in head-to-toe white and slightly hunched, an older white male motored through the halls. His big black boots shuffled along cartoonishly.

"Yes. Follow him."

The man pushed his bucket as far as the nurses' station, then left it to slide behind the desk briefly. A moment later, he moved briskly away from the camera's reach, disappearing, then reappearing on another camera's feed. He stooped to swipe a dropped cloth as Stacy exited a nearby room. Keeping his back to her, he used the rag to wipe the glass of a framed photo on the wall. Stacy barely looked up before entering the next patient's room.

"Do you recognize him?" Cole asked. "Can you zoom in on his face or ID badge? Get a better shot?"

Katie snorted. "This isn't the movies. What you see

is what we've got." She straightened her ponytail, murmuring about hospital funding and tech costs.

The janitor vanished.

"Where'd he go?" Cole barked. He pressed his palms to the workstation beside Katie, leaning closer, willing the image to reappear.

"Hang on." She went back to her keyboard, the picture of calm while Cole's heart threatened to break all his ribs. Her fingers moved at inhuman speed across the keys, sure and confident, the way Cole had felt until Rita Horn's life had collided with his. Now he saw danger everywhere. Not for him, but for her. "There."

The janitor ducked into a windowless door marked Staff.

"What is that?"

Katie leaned back in her chair, apparently satisfied with her work. "Supply closet."

When the door reopened, the man who emerged looked nothing like the old bearded janitor who'd entered. This man was tall and clean shaven, wearing a knockoff Cade County deputy's jacket and the same black boots the first image had worn.

Katie swung her face in Cole's direction. "Whoa."

The impostor strode to the nearest stairwell entry and vanished inside.

Cole snapped upright and dragged frustrated fingers through his hair. The killer himself had posed as a janitor to deliver that threat to Rita. Now he was back in faux deputy mode. Cole couldn't imagine the amount of damage a man like that could do in the guise of a Cade County deputy.

"I'm confused," Katie said. "Was that man a deputy pretending to be a janitor or a janitor pretending to be a deputy?"

"Neither." That man was a murderer. "What you've seen is part of an ongoing murder investigation." Multiple murders, attempted and successful, plus another slated to happen soon, if Cole didn't put a stop to it. "Our discussion and what you've seen here is confidential. I'm going to need a copy of this footage."

"Got it." Katie went back to work on her keyboard.

Cole ground his teeth. The jacket had shocked him with its accuracy. It was a solid facsimile, but still a knockoff. Yet someone had made a clear effort to get it right. If Cole hadn't been so intimately familiar with it, he might not have seen the small differences, either. Rita had been right to be confused by it, but knowing she'd been wrong about a fellow deputy's involvement was still an enormous relief.

Guilt rocked through him for thinking, even for a moment, that Lomar might have played a part in whatever was happening. It wasn't like Cole to doubt his team, regardless of what anyone said. This case was turning him inside out. Mentally. Physically. And emotionally.

"Done." Katie lifted a tiny plastic ninja in his direction. "I copied the footage onto my thumb drive. I included some stills of the man as the janitor and as the deputy. I'm sure your tech team could've done that themselves, but I never get to do cool stuff like this." She waved a hand in a big circle over her head. "Hospital," she added by way of explanation.

"Where did he go after the stairs?"

"I don't know. I could scan the cameras from every floor, but that would take some time. I don't know how much of a hurry you're in. Best guess, though? If he knows his way around, he probably ducked through the laundry area and into the delivery dock. Cameras are limited in those areas. People go out there to smoke because it's forbidden on hospital grounds."

"Do your cameras cover the parking lot and other exits?"

"Yes." Katie went back to her keyboard.

Cole grabbed the phone on the wall and dialed the trauma unit. The killer was on the move, but if Cole and Lomar went right now, they could cover a large portion of the perimeter in a matter of minutes, and the help he'd asked Lomar to request would be on-site before they'd finished.

The sonofagun wasn't getting away this time.

RITA STOOD AT Ryan's bedside, eyes fixed on the hallway beyond the glass. No one would get near them without her seeing them come. She'd wedged a chair beneath the doorknob and moved to her brother's side, prepared to defend him if anyone came through that door uninvited. She couldn't run if things went south, but she could fight. A number of things in the room were light enough for her to lift but heavy enough to knock an intruder out, if needed.

The coward in her said she should pull the curtain completely and hide until Cole returned. The big sister in her said that Ryan couldn't hide, so neither could she.

"You're going to be okay, Ry," she whispered to her brother's tranquil face. "I got you into this, and I'm going to get you out."

She pulled in long, steadying breaths to put the fear at bay, but the thick antiseptic scent of his room seemed heavier and more stifling with each inhalation. She couldn't afford to let emotion take over right now. She had to stay clear of thought, ready to act.

"Please wake up," she pleaded with her brother.

She stroked a line of soft hair off his forehead. If he was awake and well, they wouldn't be sitting ducks. Ryan was fast, strong and smart. He always had the best plans for getting out of trouble. She wiped a fresh tear from her cheek, remembering the antics they'd gotten into together on nights when she babysat him long ago. The way she recalled it, Ryan had also caused most of the trouble they had to get out of.

But not this. This was all on her.

She patted his arm, wrapped soundly in a long cast, then allowed herself to worry about his cast-covered leg. The one Stacy had described as *shattered*. Even if Ryan was awake, how could they hide or run from a gun-wielding, threat-rendering nut with him in such terrible shape?

Still, she just wanted her brother to wake up.

What if he never did?

Lomar strode past the window, leaving his post and making his way toward the nurses' station.

The woman in blue scrubs held a phone receiver in his direction.

Something was happening. Rita inched silently toward the glass.

Lomar stood at the nurses' station, phone to his ear. His back was to her. What was he saying? Who was on the line? Cole? Had he found something on the surveillance video?

Lomar whipped his gaze up to meet Rita's. He lifted a finger, as if to say that something would only take a minute. "Stay there," he said. His stern voice warbled through the glass.

She nodded.

Lomar ran off.

Rita's heart hammered and ached.

"Not good," she whispered. "If that call had been to announce the bad guy's capture, Lomar would've come in to tell me. Something's wrong again," she told Ryan. "I wish you'd open your eyes and tell me what to do."

Rita scanned Ryan's room for the nearest weapon.

She scooped up the paddles on a crash cart stored in the room's corner and rolled the cart into position behind the door. If anyone forced their way in, they wouldn't know she was there until she sprang on them.

She flipped the switch on the cart and watched the lights and gauges hop to life. A low hum vibrated through the room.

Business outside went on as usual.

Nurses carried clipboards and knocked on patients' doors.

Was she wrong? Could everything be fine? Rita lowered her hands to her sides. Maybe the killer had been captured. Or Cole found the janitor and he'd given him all the information Cole needed to put an end to this madness. Maybe Cole caught the janitor but he wasn't talking and he'd called Lomar to help question him. Good cop and bad cop.

There were endless possibilities, and until this week, it hadn't been like her to assume the worst.

She flicked the power switch on the crash cart to the off position and returned the paddles to their bases. The nurses weren't worried. She probably shouldn't be, either.

She gave the hallway another look. *Where were the nurses?*

Rita tugged the curtain wider in search of anyone on the floor. Maybe the woman who'd handed the phone to Lomar knew what had drawn him away.

The elevator across the hall opened for the first time in hours, and a new deputy appeared in its center.

She squinted for a better look at his face. Was he Lomar's replacement? A new shift?

Her heartbeat skittered as his thin lips curled into a sinister smile.

The killer raised his right hand, two fingers extended like a gun, and he pulled an invisible trigger.

Chapter Fifteen

Lomar's earlier call to Dispatch had sent backup to the parking lot before Cole could make it to the ground floor. That covered, he turned on his heel and headed back to Rita. Much as he wanted to be the one to capture the shooter, he hated leaving Rita alone. It seemed as if every time he took his eyes off her, things got exponentially worse.

Cole climbed the stairs as quickly as possible, struggling to move as fast as usual. The cuts and burns on his back and shoulders had begun to scream the moment he'd woken in the uncomfortable hospital chair and they hadn't stopped.

"Anything you want to tell me about the redhead?" Lomar asked, keeping pace at his side.

"No." Cole angled for position in the narrow space, eager to reach the second-floor entry.

"Really? Because you looked pretty uncomfortable in there last night."

"So?" Cole picked up the pace, injuries searing and aching with each swing of his arms.

"You don't do uncomfortable," Lomar said, "and you

sure as hell don't spend the night anywhere you don't have to. Don't say it's your job," he warned. "I was right outside the door, and another deputy could have relieved you at any time. Plus, I see the way you look at her. What's that about?"

Cole yanked the door to the second floor open and waited for Lomar to pass. "Can you blame me? She's beautiful."

"Sure, she's beautiful, but she's not your type. This one doesn't seem like the kind of woman who will put up with your shenanigans."

Cole snorted. "Leave my shenanigans alone."

He smiled at the thought of Rita's prolonged presence in his life. What would that picture look like? Would there be a ring and a big white dress in their future? She was definitely the type to wear the big dress.

Cole missed a step in the long hallway as their earlier conversation rushed back to him. Had she really implied she was a virgin?

A virgin. The words rattled nonsensically in his mind. Was that even possible?

And if it was, what did it mean for them? For starters, he'd have to take things slower than he was used to. Help her explore her sexuality. Discover what made her pant and what made her scream. A number of fun possibilities rushed to mind and *damn*! He'd never been in such a hurry to take it slow.

He shook the thought away and forced his feet to move faster, eating up the space between himself and Rita.

The first rays of sunlight had drifted in through the

wide glass windows while he was away. The nurses standing behind the desk had also changed in that time. Apparently, dawn had sent the night crew to ground.

All but Stacy.

Stacy had zipped a Rivertown hoodie over her scrubs and taken a seat in the chair Lomar recently vacated. "She's locked in," Stacy told Cole, pointing at Ryan's closed door. "She knows I'm here, but she's not opening up until she sees you."

The door cracked open. Rita peeked out. "Thank goodness."

She shoved a chair away from the door and pulled Cole inside.

The crash cart had been moved near her chair at Ryan's bedside.

"What happened?" Cole raised a hand toward the cart, but Rita intercepted it, wrapping his arm around her back instead.

She clung to him then, curling her fingers deep into the material of his shirt. "The shooter was in the elevator when the doors opened. He didn't get out, but he pointed his fingers at me like a gun."

Cole's body went rigid. "When?"

"A minute ago?" she squeaked. "Two?"

Cole swore under his breath. "We were sure he was in the parking lot, maybe even off the premises by now."

Lomar was already on his way out the door. "I'll let backup know."

Cole was torn once more. He wanted to help look for the guy threatening Rita, but he couldn't bring himself to leave her. "Listen." He lowered his mouth to her ear.

"I think it's time we get you out of here. I say we go to the station and see what Tech has recovered from that thumb drive. Put some distance between you and the killer's most recently known whereabouts."

"But Ryan..."

"Hey." Cole cut her off. "I know you're worried about him, but the way that note reads, whoever's doing this isn't going to go after you or him again until they have that pen. As long as there's a chance you're complying with their request, they're going to watch and wait."

"I can't leave him alone," she said, pushing out of Cole's grip.

"And I can't leave you." Cole worked to sound more supportive and less frustrated. Just because he didn't think someone would kill her immediately didn't mean he wasn't afraid she'd be abducted and forced to tell what she knew about the pen's whereabouts and content. "You have information they want," he continued. "Ryan doesn't. He's safe. You aren't."

Rita turned her attention back to the bed.

Cole's jaw locked and his shoulders squared. "You're coming with me because it's the right thing to do. Staying here will only keep me from helping West and the others find this guy. The longer you keep me here, the longer West is down a man, and there's only six of us to start with."

Rita gripped Ryan's fingers. "I hate this." Anger burned in her voice and eyes. "It's not fair."

"It's not," Cole admitted, "and I'm sorry." He forced himself into her line of sight. "But we can't afford to forget that you're the target. Not Ryan. Being here puts him at an added risk. He's made it through the worst. There's nothing you can do for him right now, and if he wakes while you're gone, I promise to tell him I dragged you away kicking and screaming."

Stacy climbed onto the uncomfortable chair in the corner where Cole had slept. "I could call you," she told Rita. "If you give me your number, I can send text updates. Even if there's nothing to update, I can check in periodically to say he's still okay."

Rita slumped. "My phone's in the river."

"I could text Ryan's phone." Stacy's small smile seemed to loosen Rita's shoulders. "If he had it on him before, it's probably in the envelope."

Rita's hand went to her pocket, covering the telltale outline of a cell phone. "It was. You have his number?"

"Yeah."

Rita stared at the locked screen, entered her mother's birthday, and the lock disappeared.

Lomar arrived a moment later, palms raised. He leaned against the doorjamb, defeated. "No sign of the killer."

"What do you think?" Stacy asked Rita.

Cole owed Stacy something big for calming Rita's heart. "Your shift's over," he said. "How long can you stay?"

"I'm not leaving." Stacy's smile turned sad. "I'm off for the next two days, and I plan to be here until someone kicks me out."

Rita sucked in a long breath and exhaled it slowly. "Okay. I'll keep his phone on. Promise to text me."

"Promise."

Rita kissed Ryan's cheek goodbye, then hugged Stacy before stopping at the open door and staring up at Lomar with worried and fearful eyes.

"I'll keep him safe," Lomar promised. The words rumbled low in his chest like a solemn vow. "Whatever it takes."

She flung her arms around his middle and pressed her cheek to his chest.

Lomar's eyebrows flew up. His hands hovered in the air at her back.

A long moment later, he managed to lower his arms around her narrow frame and return the embrace. He caught Cole's attention and smiled.

Seeing Rita wrapped around another man, even a man he literally trusted with his life, made Cole twitchy. Lifelong friend or not, Lomar's big mitts belonged at his sides, not on Cole's woman. He tugged the back of Rita's shirt. "Come on. Before you get him all worked up."

She released Lomar with a soft, "Thank you."

Cole twined his fingers with Rita's and led her into the parking lot, free hand on the butt of his sidearm.

RITA MADE CALLS with Ryan's phone as they motored across town in Cole's cruiser. Her neighbor had too many questions, but ultimately said Rita's cats were fine and she didn't mind watching them another day or two. Cyndi, from her office, was curious but eventually said no one else had come looking for Rita and that she should stop worrying about work and get some rest. Their dad didn't answer his phone. She left another voice mail, this one with Ryan's current status and room number. She didn't bother filling him in on the rest. It wouldn't matter, anyway.

She dropped the phone onto her lap and gave Cole a long look. He was what a man should be. Strong and steadfast, yet patient and willing to bend. "Thank you for giving me the choice to come with you."

He slid his eyes briefly in her direction. "Did I have another option?"

"You could have demanded I come and not left me any freedom of decision."

He furrowed his brow, a look of disgust on his handsome face. "Well, that's a load of manure."

A sudden smile slid over her lips. "Why?"

He glanced her way again. "Why? What? Why's it nonsense for anyone to give you orders?"

Rita shook her head. "No. You're right." Her smile widened. Cole was one of the few men who'd ever been in a position to make demands of her and he refused. He valued her opinions, choices and decisions, unlike her father, bosses, teachers and so many other men who had not. Given her current situation, Cole had every right to insist things be done his way. The fact that he didn't only made her respect him more. She turned back to the astounding autumn day blurring past her window. A cloudless blue sky played backdrop to endless multicolored mountains, thick with changing leaves. Hard to believe awful things could happen in such a beautiful place.

The sheriff's department came into view, and her heart skipped a beat. This was it. Once she delivered the pen to Memorial Park, her brother would be safe again. Hopefully the pen had already been processed for prints, the thumb drive for content, and it was ready for her.

She'd unbuckled before Cole shifted into Park.

He ran around the front of his cruiser and opened her door for her. "Ready?"

He offered her a steadying hand, then gave her fingers a squeeze.

"Yep." Rita was more than ready to finish the mess she'd started by taking that pen from the docks. What she wasn't ready for, on the other hand, was losing Cole from her life once his job was done. She'd actually like to keep him around a while if she could, but no woman held on to Cole Garrett for very long.

Though, horrific circumstances aside, she'd probably already spent more time alone with Cole than most women. Of course, the other women had probably spent a portion of their time with him naked. Ridiculously, she envied that.

Cole Garrett could undoubtedly teach her a few things.

Her cheeks flushed at the thought. Why had she told him she was a virgin? She'd never told anyone. The fact was deeply personal, and not a thing that should have been unloaded on an unreasonably attractive man she wasn't even dating. She blamed Ryan's wallet condom.

Cole opened the front door for her.

Rita tried, unsuccessfully, to untangle their fingers. They couldn't go walking into the sheriff's department holding hands like a couple. What would people think? Surely that wasn't normal. Inexperienced or not, she knew that public displays of that caliber were unofficial announcements of relationships and intimacy. Neither of those things described what she had going with Cole. *A one-sided infatuation fueled by too many emotions and time spent in close quarters.* She tried and failed to imagine him holding hands with other women. Maybe he was just an affectionate guy. Maybe he went through all the pretenses with them, too. At least until morning. "We probably shouldn't." She lifted their joined hands and wiggled them.

"Why?" Cole released the door and stepped aside. He leaned against the building's stone exterior and pulled her against him, spreading his feet to make room for hers. "You don't want to hold my hand?" He released her then, allowing her to back away.

She didn't. "It's not that."

A measure of concern lifted from his forehead. "Am I making you uncomfortable?"

"No."

He frowned. "Are you worried about what people will think?"

Silly as it was, given the much larger things she was worried about… "A little, yeah." She didn't want to be seen as some naive woman who thought she was something special to Cole Garrett. She wished it was true, but people didn't need to know that.

"Right." Cole peeled himself off the wall and straightened to his full height. He swept a hand out, indicating she should go ahead of him as they marched through the sheriff's department door.

A sharp whistle burst through the busy room almost

immediately. West waved a hand in the air, motioning for Cole to join him outside the office door. Had he been standing there waiting for their arrival?

The open door beside West had his name and title painted on it.

"Have a seat." West motioned to a pair of chairs stationed across from his desk. An open bottle of antacids sat beside a massive cup of steamless coffee near his keyboard.

Behind them, a printer rocked and grunted in the corner, spewing sheets of paper into a nearly full plastic tray.

Cole passed a small black figure to West, then hung in the doorway as Rita entered. "That's a thumb drive with hospital footage of the man we believe left the note in Ryan's things. I'm hoping our tech team can clear up the picture and identify this guy."

West curled his fist around the little ninja. "I'll get it over there."

"Thanks." Cole folded his arms and scowled at West's busy printer. "What's all that?"

"This—" West made a face at the still belching printer "—is everything from that pen you gave me. I asked Tech to fax over what they've retrieved."

Rita slid to the edge of her seat. "All of that was on the pen?"

West flopped into his chair. "Yep. And do you know how long it's going to take me to sort through it?" He answered his own question after three long beats. "Forever."

Cole approached the printer and slid a handful of pages onto his palm.

Rita rewound West's words. "So, you don't have the pen with you?"

"No," West answered. "Tech needs a couple days to make sure they have everything. I'm also hoping to find a fingerprint on it that doesn't belong to you or Minsk."

"But I need the pen," Rita said, desperation clawing at her throat. "I'm supposed to take it to the park. Show him the note, Cole."

"He's seen the note," Cole grouched. "You're not making that drop."

"Yes, I am."

His cranky face morphed into a mask of disbelief. "There is no way I'm letting that happen. How can you even think that right now?"

"What happened to letting me make my own decisions?" she asked. Hadn't he just told her not to put up with treatment like this?

"Someone has to step in when you're being irrational. I'm not going to stand by and watch you get yourself abducted or killed. Then I'd be the crazy one."

"I am not crazy," she snapped.

"Then what's your problem?"

Rita sucked air. "What is *your* problem?" She gripped the armrests of her chair, betrayal constricting her chest. This wasn't about her. "My brother is lying helpless and unconscious in a hospital room, and you want me to sit around and cross my fingers and hope the guy who put him there won't decide to walk in and kill him in his sleep? Why would I risk that when I could just do what he asked?"

Cole's chest expanded and fell in deep blasts.

"Ooo-kay." West rubbed his face with both palms. "Let's stay focused on the files for now. We can always get a replica pen, if it comes to that."

Cole swore. Loudly.

West plugged ahead, looking somewhat grayer than when Rita had met him only days before. "I need some help reviewing all these papers." He handed a thick stack to Rita from the mess on his desk. "You've been at the treasurer's office for a while now. I'm guessing you're familiar with most of these forms. I need to know who this data would be relevant to. Better yet, who does it incriminate? Who would go to such lengths to get their hands on it? So far it just looks like a bunch of bank statements and purchase offers."

Rita scooted back in her seat and crossed her legs. "If I help with this, will you let me make the drop with a fake pen?"

"Yes."

Cole grunted.

"With conditions," West added. "You're not going alone. My men will be there, in plainclothes. We'll cover the perimeter and set up takedown points throughout the park. And I'm positioning a sharpshooter on the museum roof as an added precaution." He handed Cole a sketch of what he'd described, apparently having decided on the details before Rita and Cole's arrival.

Cole looked at the drawing with profound sadness. He didn't speak.

Rita turned her eyes to the papers on her lap and went to work making sense of the documents. "These bank transfers go back a number of years."

Three days of fear and frustration fizzled and fled as her mind took hold of the familiar forms. "Wow. This is a three-million-dollar offer to buy the docks from the state." She fed the paper back onto West's desk. "Minsk must've been negotiating the purchase with the governor. I'll bet that was what had him at the municipal building so often. Is the governor in town for some reason? Or is there a liaison of some kind in Shadow Point? I'm not sure how our state government works."

"I'll make some calls," West said, "see what I can find out."

Cole paced the area beside his brother's desk. "That's going to be a problem. Politicians are practically off-limits to us. They have the power to squash an investigation before it has a chance to grow legs. They're slippery, too. Hard to get face time with them. Hard to get a straight answer, even if you do get an interview with the governor. This close to election day, we'd be wise to step extra-carefully."

West steepled his fingers. "If this is even remotely related to the governor, it would explain why the shooter has been so hard to nail down."

"Could be a professional." Cole finished his brother's thought with a solemn nod.

Rita struggled not to swallow her tongue. "A professional what? Hit man? There's a *hit man* after my brother and me?"

"We're going to have to tread lightly," Cole said, ignoring Rita's rhetorical outburst. He gathered another stack of papers and pulled a chair up beside her. "We'll have to work smart. Stay under the radar. Build our case before anyone catches wind of what we're up to. The governor won't want the media seeing our efforts to get to the bottom of this as an accusation against him."

Rita relaxed a bit, thankful to see Cole had rejoined her team.

"Who are all these bank transfers going to?" Cole asked. "Who are they from? Can Tech trace the routing numbers back to an identity on either party?"

Rita reviewed the pages, front and back. "I still don't understand why Minsk was killed. The buyer hired him to make the offers. He was the chosen liaison, so why would they want him dead?"

Cole stretched his legs out and winced. "Same thing can be said about the governor or whoever Minsk was meeting with. All the state had to do was decline or accept the offer. No grounds for murder."

Rita read several more pages, her eyes catching on a repetitive set of initials. "The letters GL appear on a bunch of these papers. Do they mean anything to you?"

"GL," Cole repeated. "Can I see it?"

He took the stack from her hands and leafed through them. "The blueprints on the boat were property of Gray Line Enterprises. Maybe that's the company that hired Minsk."

West typed something on his keyboard. "Gray Line Enterprises is a commercial development cooperative. They own docks in several large cities throughout the country."

"Louisiana, Ohio, Illinois and Missouri," Cole said. "I saw the blueprints in Minsk's office and on his boat."

Rita raised her brows. "Nothing sinister about that. What do they do with the docks they buy?"

West was silent for several minutes as he typed.

Cole leaned in Rita's direction until their shoulders bumped. "Is it the PDA you don't like? Or is it me?"

West's gaze drifted to Cole, then Rita.

"Uhm." She wet her lips and tried to slow her suddenly sprinting heart. Nothing like putting her on the spot, with an audience.

West cocked his head uncomfortably, then went back to work.

Cole shifted closer. "You don't have to be polite about it. If it's me, say it's me."

"It's not you." She whispered as softly as possible; still, the words rang through the silent little room. West's stupid printer had given up its work in time for her answer.

"If it's my reputation, we can talk about that."

Rita's cheeks flamed. "Stop. I don't care about your reputation." Caring for him scared the hell out of her, and knowing he was likely to move on the minute the case was over, thus breaking her silly heart, didn't help. She didn't care who he'd slept with before. His past wasn't any of her business. The notion his future might be, however, twisted her stomach into eager knots.

"Is it your reputation, then?" he asked.

She yanked her chin back, caught completely off guard. "What's that supposed to mean?"

West cleared his throat. "Do you two want me to leave? I mean, it's my office, but this is making me really uncomfortable."

Cole set his hand on the arm of her chair, firmly ignoring his older brother. He turned his palm up, fingers opening and closing in a greedy motion. His blue eyes danced with mischief.

West murmured something about Cole's stupidity, then continued typing.

She pushed his hand away. "I don't have a reputation."

A dare played on Cole's lips. His hand popped back into place. "But you might if you're seen with me. Is that it?"

"That's not it." Not the way Cole had meant, anyway. She just didn't want to be known as the silly girl who played at being his girlfriend when she'd already be dealing with the heartbreaking loss. "Is that why you were mad when we came in here?"

West raised both palms, eyes focused on the computer screen. "Gray Line Enterprises is listed as an import/export company. Looks like they buy unused dock space, then resell it quickly every time. In three of the locations I've searched so far, a storage facility opened within a year. Many of the secondary purchasers are the same on multiple properties."

"Shell corps?" Cole asked, returning his empty hand to his lap. "Do we know who owns the other companies? Could they all be operated by Gray Line?"

"Maybe." West lifted the receiver from his desk phone. "I'm going to pass this on to Tech Support. They'll have complete histories on all these companies before lunch. What I'd really like to know is why all the properties ended up with a storage facility."

"What do you think they're storing?" Cole asked.

Rita's tummy churned with flashes from her time on the docks. She forced her dry mouth to cooperate as she recalled the stained dress shirt and contents of the blood-splattered car trunk.

"Guns."

Chapter Sixteen

Cole pulled West's truck into the lot outside the municipal building. After Rita explained about the guns and the black sedan's bloody trunk, West had handed over his keys. The possibility of gunrunning in Shadow Point was nearly unthinkable. The fact someone in local government could be involved was worse.

He shifted the oversize pickup into Park and gave his new partner an appraising look. Bringing Rita to the place where Minsk had rendezvoused with his possible murderer was a calculated risk, but it sounded one hundred times better than letting her make that drop at the park. Cole couldn't protect her there, and he couldn't stop her from going if she put her mind to it. Worse, West had looked a little too agreeable on the matter, leaving Cole to agree to plan B.

An undercover assignment.

Rita's brows pinched in concentration. The municipal building was her turf. Cole was only there as backup, and he'd been given strict orders to lay low. Hence the vehicle swap. His cruiser would have drawn too much attention. Thanks to an unexpected night spent at the hospital, he was already deep undercover in his Army T-shirt and basketball shorts.

Rita adjusted the stack of files on her lap and took a deep breath.

"You sure you want to do this?" he asked, torn again. Wishing she'd stayed out of this, but glad to be there with her just in case there was trouble.

"I've got this." Rita pressed the passenger door open and slid into the parking lot.

Cole lowered a ball cap onto his mussed hair and went to meet her. "I've never been to the courthouse in basketball shorts."

"I don't think anyone will recognize you," Rita said. "Being out of uniform puts you out of context here, and the cap adds another layer of cover. Most people won't stare long enough to get a good look at your face. It's bad manners."

He tugged the cap lower on his forehead, curving the bill to better shade his eyes. "What about you? You're supposed to be sick. What will everyone say when they see you?"

She rolled her eyes. "People don't see me."

Cole disagreed. He followed her through Security admiring the curve of her backside in those cotton pants and trying not to make eye contact with anyone he knew.

Everything about Rita was heart-stopping sexy. How could she think no one noticed?

She paused at the bottom of the marble staircase to arrange the folders in her arms. She'd borrowed them from West's office as props. "I'm going to hit up the re-

ceptionist at the mayor's office for information. You're
·going to pretend to be visiting town and picking up lit-
erature on the area. Isla's new enough to Shadow Point
that she might not recognize you right away."

Rita hugged the folders to her chest. "Isla's an avid
gossip. I've gone out for drinks with her and Cyndi before. They talk about everyone. If there's anything juicy
available on Minsk or the mayor, or if the governor's in
town, like we guessed, Isla will know."

Hopefully Rita was right and Isla would have a significant lead. Then Rita could forget about making the
drop at the park. Everything in Cole's gut said that was
a horrible idea. "I'll be right behind you," he promised.
"Are you sure she won't know me?" Besides, the other
option was to wait outside for Rita, and that wasn't
happening.

She bit into the thick of her bottom lip. "I don't know
if Isla knows you personally, but she certainly knows
plenty about you." She started up the stairs without him.

"What do you mean?" Cole kept pace easily, attempting to look as if he wasn't speaking to Rita.

She lifted and dropped one narrow shoulder. "She's
got stories. Trust me. I've overheard more than my
share." She made a gag face, then turned for the may-
or's office.

"Hey." He grabbed her elbow without thinking. Her
eyes flashed up to meet his. There was so much he
wanted to tell her. Of course, now wasn't the time, but
for him and Rita, it was *never* the time. "I think you
and I need to talk when we finish here."

"Okay." She wiggled free of his grip. "I guess it

won't matter if she recognizes you. As long as no one realizes you're here as part of an official investigation, we're fine."

She strode through the office door, the picture of confidence.

Cole slid into the room behind her and picked up a pamphlet on the history of Cade County.

"Hi, Isla," Rita began, resting her pile of files on the reception desk.

"Rita?" Isla gasped. "I thought you were sick. You should be at home." Her eyes stretched wide. "Or at the hospital with Ryan!"

Rita's limbs twitched at the mention of her brother. Guilt contorted her features, and Cole could practically hear her wishing she'd stayed with her brother.

Come on. Don't get derailed.

"I'm trying to get by," Rita drawled, extra slow and steady, as if she were barely keeping herself upright. "I'm sick, but I'm too worried to rest or concentrate." Her voice cracked on the last word.

"You poor thing," Isla cooed.

Rita patted the folders. "I figured I'd take some work home. Maybe I can distract myself from worrying about Ryan, or at least bore myself to sleep." She slumped slightly and offered a pitiful smile, looking quite effectively put out. "I saw you here, and figured while I was in the building I might as well come and ask you about someone I've been noticing lately."

Isla popped out of her chair and leaned on her elbows over the counter. She shot Cole a curious look before turning hungry eyes back on Rita. "Who?"

"I don't even know his name." Rita sighed. "But he's tall, dark and handsome. Black hair, brown eyes, olive skin. I swear he's a Greek god or something. Always dressed to the nines. Walks like he owns everything, and sometimes I wish…" She trailed off before Isla's line of drool hit the counter.

Cole forced his fingers to ease their grip on the hunting and fishing pamphlet. Rita was improvising, and she was good.

He didn't like it.

"Well, sweetie, I'm afraid I've got bad news." Mischief crawled through Isla's eerie campfire tone. "Your man is gone. Thrown in the river." She raised her eyebrows high and waited for a reaction.

"What?" Rita pressed a hand to her collarbone, utterly overacting. "When?"

"Couple days ago. I guess you've been too sick to catch the news. His name was Roger Minsk. He used to come in and stand right where you are a few times a week."

"He did?" Rita dropped her jaw. "Why? I thought he was a lawyer or a wealthy businessman."

Isla smiled, apparently savoring the moment. "He was wealthy, all right. A land developer. Came here a bunch of times trying to make a deal about the docks."

"Oh. I hope they're finally revitalizing that area. It's been too long."

"No, now I didn't say that," Isla corrected with a glimmer of fanfare. "Roger was on a mission for some company. They made offers for the docks. He met with the mayor a few times, which is real strange because it's the governor who's in charge of that sort of thing."

"Do you think the governor was here?"

"Hell if I know. That guy's slicker than..." Isla checked over both shoulders and glanced in Cole's direction once more. "Can I help you, sir?" she asked in a sugary-sweet tone.

Cole put the pamphlet away and chose another without looking. Fly Fishing Tours. "Just seeing what your little town has to offer," he said.

"Well, honey, I don't do much fishing, but I'm guessing a man like you would have no trouble hooking a few nice ones out at Miller's pub tonight." She snapped her gum and looked pleased with herself.

"Thanks." He swapped the fishing brochure out for one on local churches.

Isla frowned. "Anyway..." She readdressed Rita in a quieter voice. "I don't know all the details on those meetings, but I can tell you that the mayor stayed late on the nights Roger was here, and he left in a big black SUV that wasn't his. I saw him from the coffee shop across the street when I was having dinner with Cyndi. We thought maybe it was a car service because he was going somewhere he shouldn't be going. Like, maybe he didn't want his car seen sitting outside the gentleman's club, you know?" She raised her eyebrows again. "I never thought that could've been the governor's driver. I'm not sure why the governor would come to Shadow Point for a secret meeting, but it makes more sense than Minsk wanting to talk to our small-town mayor about buying the docks."

"Sounds like a scandal," Rita said.

Isla perked. "I'm thinking the same thing."

Cole suspected *scandal* might be one of her favorite words.

He set his magazine aside and tipped his hat as he left the office. He'd already spent too long pretending to read tourism brochures. It was time to find a place with a good view of the office where he could wait for Rita.

RITA LEFT THE mayor's office a few moments behind Cole. She'd only been able to make her escape by telling Isla she would chase the handsome tourist into the parking lot and get his phone number.

A zip of panic raced through her when she didn't find him leaning against the wall outside the office. She headed for the staircase on quick feet, pulse beating in her ears and mind in full breakdown mode. *Cole saw the shooter and chased him. Cole was caught off guard and whisked away through the side entrance at gunpoint.*

She took a few hasty steps, and he came into view on the first floor, leaning casually against the wall and skimming her with his deep blue eyes. He trailed her with his gaze as she returned to the front of the building and exited into the sunlight. She could feel the heat of him behind her. Watching her. Following her. Dare she think it? *Wanting her.*

He followed her into the parking lot at a lumber, close enough to protect her if needed, far enough away to continue the pretense they weren't together, at least until they arrived at their destination.

He beeped the doors open when she reached West's truck and offered a hand to help her climb inside.

"That was terrifying," she told him, dropping the files onto the floorboards by her feet. "Isla's definitely already on the phone telling Cyndi I was in her office today, and Cyndi will probably have my boss on the line before I finish this sentence. I'm absolutely losing my job for playing hooky."

Cole shut her door and went to claim his position behind the wheel. He gunned the truck to life and smiled. "If Cyndi's anything like Isla, she can't tattle on you until she finds out if you got my number."

"What?" Rita smiled. "How'd you know I said I was going to?"

He laughed, shifted into Drive and pulled away from the building. "I was watching you so closely, I figured Isla would pick up on it. I didn't know you told her you were going to follow me."

Rita smiled back, enjoying the youthful expression on his too frequently distressed face.

Color bled from his cheeks at the next intersection. "Don't look now, but it seems there's a dark sedan following us."

"Where?" Rita checked the rear- and side-view mirrors.

"Three cars back." Cole pulled into the next available spot against the curb and waited. "No front plates. Dark tinted windows." He liberated his cell phone and tapped the screen to life. "We'll let him pass, then get behind him. See where he goes. Meanwhile, I'll get a cruiser out here to play sheepdog and herd him up."

The sedan slowed to a stop in the middle of the road thirty feet back. The two cars in between buzzed past their truck. The sedan idled.

Rita's heartbeat thrummed in her ears and throat. "What's he doing?" She closed her eyes and tried not to imagine the driver climbing into the street with a gun and shooting up the truck. She was with Cole now. He knew what to do. He'd handle this.

She was safe. She was safe. She was safe.

The roaring of an engine sprang her eyes wide. Squealing tires turned her on the seat.

The car pulled a U-turn on the narrow road before tearing away in a fury and peeling out of sight.

Cole returned the phone to his cup-holder. "I guess he really didn't want to pass us."

Rita rolled her window down and leaned against her door, desperate for more air.

Cole's phone rang, and he opened it on his palm. "Garrett."

"Hey." West's voice echoed through the truck cab. "Where are you?"

"I'm on Maple, and I've got you on speaker. Rita's here with me. We're finished at the mayor's office, but I just called Dispatch with the location of that sedan. It was tailing us, but it's headed in the other direction now. I'll fill you in when we get there."

West groaned.

"What do you have?" Cole asked.

"Good news and bad news," West said.

Rita lurched toward the phone. "Bad news first. Then tell us the other thing to cushion the blow."

"Well," West began, "I actually only have one thing. Good news for you, but bad news for Cole."

Cole rubbed the back of his head and swore, apparently reading his brother's mind.

"What?" she asked, leaning closer to the phone.

"I've got a decoy pen and enough men to cover the drop if you're still up for it."

She raised her determined eyes to Cole's wary ones. A wave of uncertainty threatened to steal her resolve.

Walk into a park where I know the man who keeps trying to kill me is waiting? She drew in another breath and let it out to the count of ten. She had to remember what was at stake here. If showing up at the park meant helping the killer be captured, and it would keep Ryan safe, there was nothing she wouldn't try. "Tell me when."

Chapter Seventeen

Rita dropped onto Cole's couch. She'd barely stayed on her feet while they went to pick up the decoy pen from West's office. The terrifying reality of what she'd volunteered to do was like an anvil in her gut, especially since the standard ballpoint West had given her wasn't much of a match for the actual device. With any luck, the killer hadn't gotten a good look at the original, otherwise he'd easily see her delivery for what it was. An attempt to buy time. And if they were lucky, an opportunity to draw the killer into the open for capture and arrest.

"You don't have to do this," Cole said for the fiftieth time. He'd taken a shower and changed into the luckiest pair of jeans on the planet.

"You know I do." She forced her focus to remain on his eyes, ignoring the way his soft gray T-shirt clung distractingly to his chest.

He lowered himself onto the cushion beside her and dropped fisted hands into his lap. "You've already done enough."

"I'll be fine. The plan will work," she assured him.

"Either we'll catch the killer picking up the pen after the drop, or we'll be able to follow whoever comes for it all the way back to the killer." *Assuming she had a sudden and profound change of luck.*

He cracked his knuckles, bending and stretching his fingers. A stress-release move she'd performed many times after racing deadlines. "I don't like that the property in question is owned by the state."

"Me, either."

"Or that Isla agreed the governor might be in town. Something about the way these threads are coming together is making me uncomfortable. Dirty politicians are the worst kind of criminal. They have power, money, influence and endless minions to carry out their schemes or provide alibis. This whole thing is shaping up to be a total nightmare."

"Isla could be wrong about the governor. He might have no idea Minsk exists or that our mayor was meeting with him."

Cole flicked his gaze to her. "There was three million dollars on the table, and the middleman is dead. When people have that kind of money to spend and don't get what they want, I worry."

Rita relaxed into the hard length of Cole's side and set an uncertain hand on his forearm. Ropes of hard muscle flexed at her touch, launching a thousand butterflies into her chest.

"Messing with the mayor is guaranteed to get ugly, but given what we have to go on, I don't see any way around it," Cole said. "He'll have to be interviewed, and one wrong move could ruin West's career."

Rita smiled. In the midst of everything, Cole was thinking of his brother first. She stroked the length of his arm and twined her fingers with his. "I wish we could know for sure if the governor has been in town, and if so, why." She tipped her head against Cole's shoulder, loving and hating how easy moments like these had become. How she could pick him from a crowded room in seconds, knew his voice, his touch, his presence instinctively. As if this man, a stranger only days before, had become a part of her, somehow. She snuggled closer and dragged her opposite hand over the firm muscle of his forearm. *I bet the rest of his body feels this good, too.* She imagined testing the theory inch by inch, exploring and searching, marking her arrival at each new spot with a kiss.

Cole leaned forward and caught her calves in his hands, swinging them onto his lap and forcing her back against the couch's armrest, giving her a perfect view of his face. "I've got friends in Frankfort. Maybe they can at least confirm the governor's whereabouts on the days Minsk met with the mayor." He worked his hands over Rita's calves, massaging and stroking the fatigue from her muscles.

A parade of tiny flames ignited along her skin and slowly climbed north.

"It's frustrating to have all those files from the thumb drive and still nothing to go on," he said. "What do you think is so important? What did we miss?"

"Something." Rita mentally revisited the stacks of papers from West's office. "The drop wouldn't be necessary if those papers didn't incriminate someone." But mostly the documents seemed to tell the story of a dock-buying company that wanted to buy another dock. Not exactly a sinister plot.

Cole's hands stilled on Rita's leg, one at her knee, the other slightly higher. "I don't like sending you out there without knowing who we're up against. Truth be told, I wouldn't want you out there even if we did know."

"I'll be fine," she assured him, praying that was true.

"Problem is—" he lifted pleading eyes "—I don't want you anywhere I can't be."

Breath caught in Rita's throat. "So, stay with me."

One stiff dip of his chin said he would.

His soulful blue eyes were saying something else, but Rita wasn't sure what.

Ryan's phone buzzed in her pocket with an incoming text, and she unearthed it hoping for another update from Stacy. If so, it would be the third update since they'd left the hospital.

Rita scanned the message and was relieved, once again, by the content.

"Stacy?" Cole asked.

"Yeah. No changes, but that's okay." She set the phone on the coffee table with a sigh. "I wish he'd wake up, but I'm happy to know his condition is still stable and no lunatics have paid him a visit in our absence."

"She's been on the ball about sending those texts," Cole said. "It's nice. He must be important to her."

Rita chewed her lip. Cole's statement only reminded her of the question she'd been struggling with all day. "What happens when you catch the killer?" she asked.

A growing rock of fear lodged in her throat. "I won't need a personal bodyguard anymore."

Cole's intense expression turned to surprise.

Good. He'd understood the question. When this was over, what would happen to them?

A sly smile played over Cole's lips as he raked a suddenly heated gaze over her body. "No bodyguard necessary? You sure about that?"

"Well, I've never needed protecting before," she whispered, squirming slightly under the force of his stare.

"Then who's going to protect you from me?"

Rita pulled in a sharp breath. "I don't want to be protected from you."

Cole's gaze dropped darkly to her breasts. "You sure about that?"

"Yes."

He leaned closer, sliding one broad palm beneath the back of her shirt and splaying strong fingers against her bare skin. Her back arched slightly in response. "You took a strong No PDA stance at the sheriff's department. I believe you said you were concerned about how your reputation would be impacted if you're seen with me. You want to talk about that?" He turned his eyes to her body as his free hand skimmed across her ribs, thumb grazing the thin fabric of her shirt and raising her nipple to attention.

The heat of embarrassment rushed over her cheeks and throat, but Cole's lids drooped hungrily over the change he'd created in her.

"I know your reputation," she said, doing her best

to keep her eyes from closing under the extreme pleasure of his touch.

"And you're worried I'm going to walk away because that's what I always do," he guessed. "You think my interest in you will end soon."

"I'm worried about how silly I must look for wishing that wasn't true."

Cole's gaze met hers. His jaw set. His hands stilled. "You don't look silly to me. You look like everything I never realized I wanted, and I want it bad."

"Kiss me," she whispered, desperate to have him closer. "Please?"

Rita arched farther, rising up to meet him. He was too far away, unfairly watching as her body reacted to the slightest of his touches. She wanted more, and if this was the end for them, the last of her time with the most amazing man she'd ever known, then maybe it was time to make the most of it. "Don't stop touching me."

Cole hovered over Rita in one quick move, legs fixed between hers on the narrow couch. He teased her cheeks and jaw with the tip of his nose and the scruff of his chin, leaving a haze of himself on every inch of her face, neck and ears. His expert hands continued their work on her begging breasts.

"Cole." She panted and was rewarded with the sweet taste of his mouth on hers.

He deepened the kiss slowly, intoxicatingly, lowering his body against her until she felt the hard press of him between her thighs.

She ruined the kiss with a ragged gasp for air. Unable to resist, she lowered her hand to his jeans in disbelief, shocked and a little concerned by the size of him.

"Everything okay?" he asked, pulling back for a look at her face.

"You're huge," she stated flatly, contemplating the possibility of losing her virginity to Cole Garrett, a man she admired as much as she desired.

A small light of clarity flashed in Cole's lust-filled eyes. He bumped against her palm with a groan. "I can't believe I'm saying this, but maybe now isn't the right time." His voice was low and hot with need, but tempered by restraint. "We can take it as slow as you want." He traced the ridge of her ear with his tongue.

Her hips rocked against his. "Maybe just a little more?" This might not be the right time for sex, but she certainly had a few questions she'd like answered. "Can you show me how to touch you?"

Cole swept her wrists over her head and pinned them to the couch. "Not tonight." He left a path of wet kisses along her jawline and down her throat to her collarbone where he suckled the tender skin into gooseflesh.

He released her wrists in favor of dragging her shirt over her head and tossing the garment onto the floor. Cole's warm mouth lowered to the spot where her nipple tested her bra, and he rolled his eyes up to her again in question. One skilled finger slid beneath the thin material, tightening her skin impossibly further.

Rita curled her fingers into the thick of Cole's hair and moaned with indescribable need. "Please."

With a pinch of his fingers, the clasp at her back was released. He swept the flimsy material of her bra away and cradled her bare breasts in his hands. His tongue passed over his lips as he pulled one budded tip into his mouth and lavished it with tender care.

Helpless against the raging fireworks inside of her, Rita bent her knees to grip his hips and arched deep into his mouth. "Cole." She moaned the word, her body squirming, begging for more.

He pulled his shirt over his head and flung it onto the growing pile of their discarded clothing. The heat of him, the clean, freshly showered scent of him, the feel of his hot skin on hers was nearly too much, and he threatened to undo her with each flick of his tongue. Cole was everywhere and yet not close enough.

"More," she whispered, clinging to him with a desperation she'd never known.

Cole's hand toured the contours of her stomach, gliding lower until his fingers vanished beneath the silk of her panties.

"Oh!" Her knees fell wide as he explored the depth of her. Slowly at first, then suddenly more than she could stand. The sensation rode through her like a crashing wave, twisting her hips and drawing out a long, breathy moan of ecstasy.

Rita opened heavy, satisfied eyes, enjoying the prickles of pleasure still coursing over her sweat-slicked skin. He'd barely touched her and yet…

Still stroking and petting her heated skin, Cole watched as she fell from the climax. He closed his lips over hers in a kiss that nearly made her see stars.

"More." She breathed the word against his lips.

Cole pulled back with a deeply satisfied smile. "Baby, I haven't even gotten started."

COLE HAD WATCHED the tension melt off Rita's face in an explosion of shock and delight. *That's amazing*, she'd whispered, utterly out of breath from a tidal wave of orgasm. It was wrong, and more than a little caveman-esque, but his chest had puffed with pride at the accomplishment. She'd offered him full access to her body and he'd signed those papers in full, delivering her first *and second* orgasms in slow, erotic procession. Whatever else she ever did with any man, those milestones belonged to him. And so did the stubble marks left over every inch of her naked body.

He ground his teeth at the thought of another man near her like that.

Not on his watch.

On his watch, Cole had coaxed her into pieces with the slip of his tongue and skill of his hand, assuring her virginity remained intact, despite her best efforts at handing it over. Which, he hoped, would prove just how much she could trust him.

Cole double-, then triple-checked West's plan for the pen drop while Rita dozed peacefully on his couch. She'd barely slept while they were at the hospital, and he'd done his best to wear her out before slipping away to get them both a glass of ice water. She'd been out like a light when he'd returned.

He hated to disturb her, but they needed to leave for the park soon, so reluctantly, he woke Rita with a soft kiss. "Hey."

A blush crept over her skin. "Hi."

He scooted himself onto the couch in the curve of her narrow figure, careful not to sit on the quilt he'd covered her with. "West says our team will be in place within the hour. Any chance I can talk you out of this?"

She wiggled upright, pulling the quilt with her. "About earlier," she started.

He caressed her flushed cheek with the backs of his fingers. "We should probably talk about that, huh?" They had talked about it, technically, if he counted her begging for more, and his saying yes. Well, eventually, she'd been the one saying *yes*, but he'd given her all he could without crossing the line. Not today. Cole was taking it slow for her. He fought a proud smile.

She averted her gaze, cheeks bright red. "I don't normally do that sort of thing. I mean, we haven't known each other long. We aren't dating." She bit her lip and shut her eyes. "With you, my mind just…" She waved her hands around her head in a little typhoon.

He knew exactly what she meant. "We can talk now," he suggested, struggling to push the sound of her calling his name from his mind.

"No." Rita practically jumped off the couch, clutching the blanket to her remarkably sexy figure. "I should shower now." She baby-stepped backward, away from him.

Cole climbed off the couch and followed her. One step forward for each of her steps back. "Are you upset?"

"No."

"Am I making you uncomfortable?"

"No."

"You sure? 'Cause it looks like you're running away."

She shook her head hard in the negative. "Nope."

He felt his face wrinkle in confusion, mentally seeking a reason for the sudden and drastic change. "Are you embarrassed for some reason?" Hadn't the naked time proved she was implicitly comfortable with him?

"I'll only be a minute." She turned and disappeared into his bathroom.

And that made twice in the last two hours he'd missed a perfect opportunity to tell her he was falling in love.

THE PARK WAS crowded with families when they arrived. Strolling couples, swinging children, people flying kites and throwing balls. Joggers. Bicyclists. Everyone seemed to be out enjoying the final moments of the day.

Above it all, the pale blue sky was dashed with streaky white clouds and fading slowly into the amber shades of a setting sun.

Rita tugged the belt on her white wool coat a little tighter. Her thick red hair was tied back in a messy bun.

Cole kept the hood of his navy sweatshirt pulled carefully over his head, enough to hide his face without fully obstructing his view of their surroundings.

With any luck, the two of them looked like a normal couple out enjoying a walk.

He slid a protective arm behind Rita's back and spoke softly as they moved toward the mailbox. "Do you see the man with the big black dog? That's Lomar," he said. "The suit on the bench reading the paper? Deputy Franks. Hospital security is watching your brother, and I can identify all the men on my team from here. You're in very good hands." He tugged her closer and planted a kiss on her cheek. "See the tall Ken-doll-looking guy over there? The one pretending to talk on the phone? That's my brother, Blake. He's not even part of the sheriff's department. He's FBI, and he can't resist the chance to take down a bad guy."

"FBI? So you're all in law enforcement?"

"Like I said, it's in the blood. Blake married a local nature photographer and moved home last year. He'd been away for a long time before that, dealing with his demons, I suppose. Now he can't seem to stop offering his services." Cole smiled. Both Blake and West had recently fallen in love and it had changed their lives irrevocably.

Cole had even made his share of jokes at Blake's and West's expense on the matter, and now he had plans to follow their lead if Rita would have him.

He gathered her into his arms when they reached the mailbox. Before she could crouch to make the drop, he had something to say.

She looked up at him, clearly startled. "What are you doing?"

"I don't want to find another reason to put this off," he said. "I like what we have here, and regardless of what happens with this case, I don't want us to end."

Her mouth twitched. "Me, either."

"Yeah?"

Rita nodded.

"Don't leave when the case is closed," he told her, a little more sternly than he'd intended.

"Never." She rocked onto her toes and kissed him like she meant it.

Warmth bloomed in his chest. He caught her wrists in his hand and hooked them around his neck, dragging her body more tightly against his. Cole had been with lots of women who didn't matter. He'd never been with one who truly did, and the feeling, he realized, was like a drug. "While you're feeling so agreeable," he said. "I'd like it if you'd have me. And only me." He'd seen her fall apart in his hands today, and the moment had wrecked him for other women forever. He didn't want any man to ever see her like that. That was just for him.

A smile budded on Rita's lips. "Back at ya." She released him after a small kiss and extended her hand to seal the deal with a handshake.

Cole chuckled, accepting the terms. He rubbed the goofy smile off his lips as Rita crouched beside the mailbox to leave the decoy pen. He'd surely hear about the scene that had played out publicly between them from every single member of his team when this was over.

Rita brushed her palms together. "Done."

"Good. Now let's get the hell out of here." He gripped her tiny hand in his and turned back the way they'd come.

A sharp glint of light stopped him midstride. "Did you see that?"

"What?"

He turned in a slow circle, scanning building tops and shadowed spaces. "A flash. Like light bouncing off a..."

The gunshot cracked through the air, drowning out his voice and scattering people in every direction.

Children cried. Mothers screamed.

Cole swore.

"Get down! Get down!" The familiar voices of his brothers and fellow deputies echoed through the air. "Get down!"

Cole yanked Rita's arm. "Run!"

They broke into a sprint, hands knotted together.

"Straight to the truck," he yelled over the deafening din of panic in the air.

Another shot exploded. Closer this time, blasting a divot of grass before them.

Rita screamed again, digging her feet into the ground and looking like she had on the boat when she'd seen the bomb ticking so close to zero.

"You can do this," he whispered, and her feet began to move again.

Cole cursed himself internally. He'd been blind, thinking only of Rita's safety and his feelings for her. He hadn't taken the time to scrutinize the situation. If he had, he would've realized it was a setup. "This wasn't about the pen," he snapped, overcome with frustration and terror as men and women rushed around them in every direction, making it impossible to get eyes on any of his team members without slowing their run. Hopefully at least one of the good guys had them covered.

This drop had never been about regaining the thumb drive. Nothing on those documents had pointed fingers directly at anyone. No, someone had wanted Rita out in the open, and this was a plot to get rid of the last witness.

Chapter Eighteen

Cole's ears roared with excess adrenaline as he barreled away from the park. How had he not seen the drop for what it really was? An ambush.

Screaming sirens and flashing lights seemed to fill the already thin air as ambulances rushed by them in the opposite direction, pushing traffic onto the berm. A bleating firetruck made Rita turn in her seat, trailing it with her eyes as it disappeared behind them. "Someone called 911," Cole said, by way of explanation. "Probably a witness or bystander." A citizen wouldn't have known that everyone in local law enforcement was already on-site with the shooter. If West or a deputy had made the call for emergency responders, however, it could only mean someone needed an ambulance.

He dragged his phone from his pocket and dialed West on speaker.

He'd put a few miles between Rita and the gunman with no signs of a tail. It was time to check in.

"You okay?" West answered without a greeting.

"Yeah. You?"

"Yeah. Rita?"

Cole slid his eyes toward the trembling woman at his side. "She will be. We saw the ambulances. Anyone hurt? Tell me you caught this guy."

"Nah," West huffed into the receiver. "The guy is vapor. We've fanned out to see if he's still here, maybe trying to blend in, but we've got nothing. Thankfully, no one was injured, but there's no way around a press conference now."

Cole eased the gas pedal off the floor.

"Shooter at a local park." West exhaled the words. "This was bad. And, man, I hate reporters. Luckily, the team's all here."

Was it lucky? Or just shameful that they were all on-site and no one had been able to prevent a public shooting? Cole grimaced. West would be doing public relations cleanup for the rest of his time behind the badge after this.

He rocked his head side to side, stretching the bunched muscles along his neck and shoulders. "And no sign of the gunman?"

"Not yet."

Rita leaned closer to the phone on Cole's open palm, her hands fisted over the material of her coat sleeves. "What about the pen?"

"Gone."

Her pale face went impossibly whiter. "Did he open fire because he realized what I'd done? That I'd delivered a fake?" She flicked her terrified gaze to Cole. "I broke the deal."

"Don't do that," West said. "This isn't on you. The pen was in place at the time of the first gunshot. We lost track of it after that, while we herded folks to safety. When we went back, it was gone. It's possible the shots were meant for that purpose. To distract us."

Cole set the phone on his thigh and reached for Rita with one hand. "What if this was never about the pen? What if the drop was designed to get Rita out in the open? It created an opportunity to eliminate the only person who can identify both men from the docks that night."

"I didn't see both men," Rita said, shaking her head. "Only the one who chased me."

"They don't know that," Cole argued. "From what you've told us, those men have no idea how long you were standing in the shadows. You could've been there when they arrived, could've seen and heard everything that went on, and now you're spending a lot of time with cops."

Rita fell back against the seat, her breath whooshing free in a deep exhale.

Cole could practically see the guilt-ridden thoughts running through her head. "This is not your fault." He gripped her hand. "Hey."

Her sweet hazel eyes glistened with unshed tears.

"It's not," he promised.

"But if I hadn't insisted on coming…"

"No." West's voice cracked through the air, startling Cole.

It was so easy to forget everything else when she was there.

"This is not your fault," West said. "None of it. Not his stalking you, not your brother's accident and not the shooting at the park. Whatever this psychopath does, he's doing it by choice. *His* choice. *His* agenda. You are not to blame for his crimes, regardless of how your anxious heart twists the facts. You got it? Because I want you to hear that. Really understand it."

Cole smiled. He'd seen his fun-loving brother in boss mode more times than he could count, and there was no denying him anything when he got like that. Another reason he made a great sheriff. West could put people at ease without feeling obligated to be their best friend. He got the job done. All of it. And folks respected him for it.

Rita released a long slow breath. "You're right. I need to stay focused."

"Atta girl," West said, his voice going easy and kind. "Cole. Why don't you take Rita somewhere safe while we finish the witness interviews and scan the park? I want to visit some of the nearby buildings for signs the shooter was there. If we know where he waited for her, it could give us another clue about who he is. If he has ties in the area, professional training, anything like that, I can follow it back to him. Lomar's collecting the spent rounds. That'll help, too."

Cole nodded at the phone. "I saw a glint of light before the first shot. Could've been sunlight off a rifle scope."

"Where?"

"East of the mailbox, between the drop location and the parking lot. We were headed back to the truck. A rooftop maybe."

"Good," West said, a rumble of pride in his voice.

"That's what we need. Something to go on. You get your lady to safety, and I'll call when we have something."

Rita turned, fear overtaking her pretty features. "Can I see my brother?"

Cole stopped at the next intersection, waiting for West to chime in. Cole was definitely against a trip to the hospital, but West could deliver the bad news this time. He wasn't the one trying to keep her both safe and happy. A more and more difficult task, given their circumstances.

Rita made a pleading face at Cole. "I don't want anyone to go after Ryan again because of what I just did. The note said to bring the pen to the park. I didn't. I brought a fake. The note said to come alone. I didn't. I brought the whole sheriff's department. Ryan's unconscious in the trauma ward. He's helpless and alone. His only protection is a crew of nurses and hospital security. I have to see him."

"Can it wait?" West asked. "Hospital security has the entire floor locked down, and I trust them. I'd prefer you postpone your next visit until a deputy can go with you."

"Hey." Cole glared at the windshield, easing through the intersection, half expecting the dreaded black sedan to appear in his rearview. "I'm with her. *I'm* a deputy."

"Yeah, and when was the last time you slept?" West asked.

Cole ground his teeth. "Last night."

"For how long?"

Cole pursed his lips.

"I'm guessing it wasn't long," West said, answering his own question with undeniable self-importance. "And correct me if I'm wrong, but whatever insufficient amount of sleep you got was on the same day you were knocked unconscious after leaping off a boat that exploded." He broke the final word into syllables. "Am I right? And I heard Uncle Henry tell you to rest and take something for the pain. Did you do either of those things? Really? Have you even changed the bandages?"

"Are you serious with this right now?" It was one thing to be perpetually teased for being the baby of the family, and completely another to be told he wasn't fit to protect Rita and Ryan until another deputy arrived. "I can do this."

"Of course you can," West said, managing to sound exasperated despite the fact he'd started this. "I know you can. You, out of all of us brothers, always could do damn near anything. But it doesn't mean you should. And it's a proven fact that fatigue wrecks your ability to think on your feet and it slows your reflexes. Would you want anyone else in your condition protecting Rita and her brother? Or do you want to stow your stubborn pride, stop trying to prove something to everyone all the time and just wait until a deputy who's slept longer than four hours in the last two nights gets there to help?"

Cole traded his hold on Rita for a double fisted grip around the steering wheel. He hated to admit it, but West's reasoning was strong, and throwing Rita's safety into the argument made it impossible to disagree. "I'm not trying to prove anything," he said, already defeated. He would wait for the next deputy to arrive before taking Rita to the hospital.

"You are." The zeal had washed from West's voice. "You always have been, but you never needed to. Do me a favor, as your brother, not your boss. Take Rita to Grandpa's cabin or Mom and Dad's place, find a bed with a blanket in a room with a locking door, then get some sleep. I need you healed up and ready to go. We can't do this without you."

Pride stung Cole's throat. "Yes, sir." He closed the phone and set it in the cupholder, unable to look in Rita's direction. He was nearly thirty years old, and his brother's approval never stopped feeling like he'd just won the middle-school fishing derby.

Rita reached for his hand on the wheel and pulled it onto her lap. "That was nice."

Cole laughed. "Yeah. That wasn't bad."

"He's proud of you," she said. "Didn't sound to me like he thinks you're not enough. It sounded to me like he's an older brother."

Cole cleared his throat, not trusting his voice to sound as strong as he needed it to be for her. "Ryan's going to be just fine, but we can head over there whenever you're ready. I'll leave that up to you."

She shook her head. "No. West's right. It can wait. I've still got his phone. Stacy's updates are still coming steady and strong. I know he's safe. His condition hasn't declined, and he's in good hands. I don't want to lead any more danger Ryan's way. How far away is your grandfather's cabin?"

"About twenty miles. A forty-minute trip from here. Lots of back roads and rough terrain. I haven't been there in years, but it's secluded. Not many people even know it's there." He veered right at the next fork in the road, angling away from shops and local residences onto a narrow finger that would soon be made of mud and gravel.

"Sounds perfect," she said. "I'll call Stacy when we get there and let her know we'll be back tonight unless she needs us sooner. I wouldn't mind a verbal update, either. Texts are nice, but I'd like to hear her tell me he's okay."

Cole watched as she swiveled forward, turning her body back to face the windshield. Was it wrong of him to feel so much pride in knowing her? Her strength of will. Her love for family. Was it wrong of him to want her to be a part of his life permanently, and as soon as possible?

She lifted her sweet-spirited smile to him, light and pure in a moment of sheer perfection. Things were going to be okay.

"Cole." Her eyes went suddenly wide, and Cole followed her gaze though his driver's-side window as a giant truck slammed into his door. Metal twisted and crunched. Glass shattered over them. Cole's arms flew away from the wheel, and his torso jerked toward Rita like a rag doll, thrust away from the caved-in door.

Rita's piercing scream was cut short as their truck rocked briefly onto two wheels before slamming back onto the ground.

The massive tow truck reversed away from them and stopped.

Cole fumbled for the steering wheel and gas pedal. His truck didn't respond.

The silver beast stopped retreating at twenty feet away and shifted loudly with powerful bursts of torque. Broad black tires crept toward them like a predator.

Cole cranked the ignition with all his might. The thing was going to run them over. "Rita?"

She was slumped against the passenger door, unmoving and covered in pebbles of busted glass.

"Rita!"

The angry squealing of tires drowned his best efforts to wake her as the attacking truck raced forward once more.

The resulting collision sent Cole rolling into darkness.

RITA WOKE TO the steady pounding of her head and throbbing of her shoulder. Her hands dangled over her head thanks to the topsy-turvy position of Cole's truck. She struggled to make sense of her new view.

They'd been in an accident!

Beside her, Cole hung limply in his safety belt, fingers resting on the ceiling, trickles of blood racing in crimson rivulets from the gash on his chin, climbing over his nose and closed eyes to his forehead. "Cole!"

She reached for him, uselessly, unable to make contact. Her arms were too short and her seatbelt unforgiving. Pain flashed through her head in bursts of blinding light.

Suddenly, the door at her side swung open with a sickening groan.

"Help him first," she called. "Help the driver. He's not moving. There's blood!"

A man in a deputy's jacket lowered onto his knees outside the open door. "Hello, Trouble," he said.

"Cole!" Rita screamed as the shooter reached for her with black leather gloves. He held her easily in place as he sawed through her seat belt with a giant pocketknife.

Cole's eyelids flickered open as her restraint broke free, dropping her onto her head in the upside-down cab. Her legs and feet crashed over her, connecting sharply with the dashboard and the side of Cole's face.

"Rita." He choked out her name.

Tears blurred her vision. "Help." She forced the word out, knowing there was no help for her. This was it. The killer had won.

Cole swung an arm in her direction, then called out in pain. "No!"

Her assailant shoved his head through the open door and clamped leather-clad fingers around her arms, jerking her roughly toward him. "Time to say goodbye."

Rita scrambled to tether herself to anything, but the jagged shards of broken glass tore through her tender flesh with each desperate move.

"Rita!" Cole struggled behind her, swearing and yelping as he worked to unlatch his seat belt.

"Gotcha." The attacker locked his hands beneath her armpits and hauled her into the rays of the setting sun.

She screamed and fought as he dragged her along the road toward the black sedan parked nearby.

A driverless tow truck sat empty beside Cole's pickup, its bumper lying on the ground below a cracked and broken grille.

In the distance, a man in unmarked coveralls climbed into the passenger side of another sedan.

"How many of you are there?" Rita asked, suddenly realizing that today's shooter may have been someone else entirely. "Are you the one who almost killed my brother? Did you leave the note at the hospital?"

He wound an arm around her ribs and pulled her tight against his chest, pressing the air from her lungs. With his free hand, he produced a black key fob.

The sedan's trunk popped open and memories of the blood and guns rushed back to her. This time, the space was empty but lined in heavy plastic.

"I'm not getting in there," she insisted, applying every self-defense technique her father had taught her for getting away. Unfortunately, her fuzzy head and wobbly limbs rendered her efforts useless.

He shoved her forward with a jolt, pressing her thighs against the car's open trunk and himself against her backside.

"No!" The pressure of his body forced upon her sent Rita into desperation.

He leaned harder into her, forcing her body to jack-knife. One gloved hand covered her mouth, the other was anchored against the plastic-lined trunk floor, leaving her no room to fight and no hope of escape. "Get in." Hot, stale breath washed over her face, sickening her further as she tried not to think about the way his body assaulted hers.

"No."

In one shocking heave, Rita was off her feet and on her back inside the cramped space of the sedan trunk.

Scents of carpet cleaners and stain removers bit at her nose and eyes. She clawed at his gloves and jacket as he held her down, wishing she could somehow fill her fingernails with his DNA or at least a useful thread to hang him by when her body washed up at the river tomorrow morning. "Don't do this," she cried. "You don't have to do this."

The man gave a final shove, expelling the oxygen from her lungs once more, then reaching for the trunk lid. "Yes. I do."

Chapter Nineteen

The space inside the trunk was hot and confined. Mixed with the strong chemical scents and darkness, Rita's head screamed for mercy. She traced the trunk with trembling hands, searching for the escape button, but the emergency release handle inside the trunk had been disabled. She couldn't help wondering if Minsk had taken this same ride to his death. Had he gone through the same motions? And, if so, how could she survive if he hadn't?

To make matters impossibly worse, there was nothing available that she could use as a weapon when the car finally stopped. The trunk held not a single item other than her and the plastic, slick with sweat beneath her palms.

Think. She pressed her fingertips hard against both temples and squeezed her eyes shut for clarity. If the car stopped, she could scream for help, pound on the trunk and hope someone heard her, maybe another car or a jogger. So far, the car had barely slowed.

Rita rolled into the fetal position, fighting against the rising panic. A pinch at her hip sent her heart aflutter with new hope. Ryan's phone! Her aching, terrified, addled mind had forgotten the most obvious of tools. A literal help line.

She wiggled the device from her pocket and swiped the screen to life. The backlight burned her eyes, and she squinted against the sudden pain. Rita dialed the only number she could think of, the one she'd memorized just days before. Cole's cell phone.

Her call went to voice mail.

His phone, like hers, was at the bottom of the river.

She didn't know the number to Cole's flip phone.

Nine-one-one. She dialed the new number with growing hope.

"Nine-one-one," a raspy female voice answered. "What's your emergency?"

"This is Rita Horn." She nearly sobbed the words. "I'm in the trunk of a car. I was taken from an accident. Cole Garrett is hurt." Her rambling thoughts spilled through trembling lips.

"Ma'am," the voice interrupted. "You're breaking up. What's your emergency?"

Rita swallowed a whimper. Her bubble of hope nearly gone. "I've been abducted," she screamed the words. "Help me!"

"Miss Horn?" The strange voice perked. "Rita Horn?"

"Yes! Yes. It's me. We were in an accident. I don't know where I am."

"I'm patching you through to the sheriff."

Rita wiped her eyes. Scents of motor oil and exhaust seeped into her senses, mixing with the heat and chemicals, churning her stomach into a vortex.

"Rita?" West's voice crackled through the line.

"Yes!" The Garretts would save her. They were a pack of small town superheroes. She was going to be okay. *Everything would be okay.*

"I can't hear you," he said, an edge of frustration in his voice. "Can you hear me?"

"Yes!"

"If you can still hear me, stay on the line. I won't hang up. We're starting a trace now. Cole's on his way to the hospital." West's voice cut out. The air went still. Background noise and rustling wind through the receiver. Gone. Snatched away when she needed them most.

"West?" She jerked the phone away from her ear and stared in disbelief.

The phone's timer ticked upward, tracking silent seconds as the call continued, her ability to communicate gone.

Tears poured over Rita's cheeks.

Cole was going to the hospital. What if he was badly hurt? What if his injuries were worse than she'd imagined? What if he was seriously, permanently injured, or worse?

The steady hum of the sedan's tires on pavement eventually changed into the loud crunching of gravel, and the mostly smooth ride grew intensely rough and bone rattling.

She gritted her teeth against the pain as her aching body jostled and bounced inside the hot trunk. Rita listened closely as the car's engine soon settled and a door opened and shut. Footfalls ground through the rocks outside before a quick beep released the trunk lid.

Rita slid the phone up her coat sleeve and curled her fingers around the hidden device. She shut her eyes and went limp.

Sunlight rushed over her face. The sharp golden glow was a hammer to her throbbing head. "Wake up," the man growled.

Rita feigned a coma. Dead weight was harder to carry, and he couldn't force her onto her feet again if she was unconscious.

"Come on." Angry hands circled her biceps and yanked her upright.

She let her head loll over one shoulder, determined to pull off the con. If she was lucky, he'd skip shooting her and simply toss her into the river where she'd have a fighting chance.

The man leaned closer and patted her cheek sharply, stinking up the already rank air with his nasty breath. Wherever they were, it didn't smell like the docks. It smelled like manure.

"Up you go." He jammed his shoulder into her ribs and tipped her over him like a sack of potatoes.

"Stop!" Rita screamed and kicked, realizing her plan to slow him down by being still was foiled by her small size.

New plan. She thumped his back with both fists and wailed into the endless countryside.

"Hey!" he shouted. "Knock it off or I'll knock you out."

Rita went still. Her chest heaved with desperation.

Could West hear her pleas through the phone tucked up her sleeve? How long could she hold on to her lifeline before the caveman beneath her took it away?

She let her lids close on a silent prayer, then gave one more wild round of squeals and kicks. When her assailant began to threaten and complain, she released the cell phone, aiming it toward the sedan.

Ryan's phone collided with the gravel and bounced before rolling to a stop beneath the car.

"What are you doing?" He flipped her off his shoulder, wrenching her arm behind her back and surely dislocating her shoulder. "Walk!" He gripped her neck with hot, meaty fingers and shoved her forward along a dirt path.

Rita strained for a better view of her surroundings. Where was the river? Everywhere she looked were overgrown fields and rolling hills of long-abandoned farmland. An armless scarecrow hung cockeyed on a wooden stake, impaled long ago and left to guard against nothing but the wind.

There would be no chance of swimming to shore now. No chance at surviving or being found. They weren't at the river. They were in no-man's-land.

A dilapidated old barn rose on the fiery horizon, its weathered boards dark with age and neglect. Its concave roof gaped with a hole the size of a tractor.

"You don't have to do this," she said, trying those words again as she dug her feet into the hardened earth.

The man shoved her forward in giant bursts of force, eventually knocking her through the yawning doorway and into the ominous structure.

Rita batted her eyes, adjusting to the dimmer light. The sinking sun bathed the space in eerie shades of crimson and scarlet, casting long shadows over the floor and illuminating dust motes like falling embers ready to set her world ablaze.

Bits of ancient hay swirled along the ground, caught in the breeze blowing in from the field. Dirt and animal hair floated in the air, peppering her senses with the overwhelming scents of death and decay. A rickety wooden chair stood in the room's center.

The man stepped away then. He removed a handgun from beneath his jacket and pointed it at her middle. "Sit."

Rita stopped. "Cole will find me," she warned. And he would.

Though whether he'd find her alive or dead was yet to be known.

"I don't think so." Her abductor smashed one large palm hard against her shoulder, eliciting a yelp and successfully bending her knees. The chair rocked with the shock of her collapse upon it. "He was a little tied up last I saw him."

"Then the sheriff will find me," she said, "or another deputy, another Garrett, but someone will come, and you'll pay for the things you've done." Newfound bravery worked through her core and pushed free of her lips. She had nothing to lose, and delaying her death might mean saving her life.

He kneeled beside her and produced a length of rope. "Quiet."

Rita slid her hands deep into her sleeves and gauged

the distance to the barn door. Her mind raged with impossible questions. Could she outrun him? Would he shoot her if she tried? Was she willing to find out? "You should let me go and spend your time getting out of town before you're arrested. This could be your last day as a free man. Is killing an office clerk really how you want to spend your time?"

"Not really. Hands behind your back. Unless you want a hole in your forehead like the others."

The others. Like Minsk and his poor maid.

Rita dropped her arms at her side. "My shoulder," she winced, biting into the thick of her lip. "I think it's out of the socket. I can't move it any farther."

He yanked it back for her.

She screamed in agony. Black dots danced before her eyes and her stomach rolled. "I'm going to be sick."

"You'll feel better soon." He tightened thick scratchy rope around her wrists with speed and precision.

"Why are you doing this?"

He rose to his feet and stared blank-faced at her for a long beat. "Family."

Family? What did that mean? "Well, you don't have to. Whoever's making you do these things is just using you, and you can stop. The Garretts can help you."

He blinked through a sudden look of remorse. "No one can help me."

"Give us a minute." A long shadow stretched toward them. The slow Southern drawl crawled over Rita's skin. "Finally, we meet."

Her abductor tucked the gun into a holster on his

side and walked out the way he'd come in, giving the new arrival a wide berth.

Curiosity and defiance stiffened Rita's spine and narrowed her eyes.

The newcomer was tall and broad, a faceless silhouette. The waning light rode slowly over him with each new step, illuminating shiny black shoes, then gray suit pants and a dress shirt that stilled Rita's heart. His shape and stride confirmed her worst nightmare. This was the man with the bloodstains on the docks.

"Hello, Miss Horn." He tipped his head in greeting.

"You," she seethed. This was the man pulling the strings. The one who'd called the shots that nearly killed her brother. And Cole. And her.

"Who are you?" she asked. He wasn't the mayor or the governor; she'd easily recognize both, and he was neither. "What do you want from me?"

"I tried to scare you off," he said. "Tried everything, but nothing worked. You had to show up that night. Become a witness. Steal evidence, then run. You stopped going to work. Stopped going home. If only you would have cooperated."

Rita squinted at the middle-aged stranger. There was something familiar in the line of his jaw. The set of his eyes. Had they met before?

"You really don't know who I am?" he asked.

"A sociopath?" she guessed.

He pulled his chin back, looking significantly put off by her answer. "Think harder, Miss Horn. You work at the municipal building, don't you?"

Her jaw dropped. Recognition hit like a bat to the

forehead. "Senator Sayers?" She'd walked by his portrait, hanging beside the ones of the president and governor, many times a day for several years.

He smiled. "See. I knew you were smart."

So, they had been right to suspect an elected official's involvement. They just hadn't thought far enough up the food chain.

Rita shored up her nerve and prayed to look more composed than she felt. Something about the senator told her that he'd have little patience for a panicking woman who shed tears and begged forgiveness. "Why are you doing this?"

"You wouldn't understand."

"Try me." Rita forced back the bile pooling in her throat. Pain, fear and nausea circled in her gut and lightened her head by the minute. Scents of rotting wood and hay stirred with sunbaked animal hair and excrement. It was only a matter of time before she was sick or passed out.

If it came to that, would he kill her while she was unconscious?

The senator chuckled. He locked his hands behind his back and looked briefly at the ceiling, as if debating where to begin.

"I'm sure you weren't always like this," she prompted, her voice warbling with fear.

"I made a bad decision ten years ago." He stared past her, apparently lost in thought. "Sometimes it's impossible to put bad things behind us."

"What kind of bad decision?" she asked, hoping to

stall the inevitable. Rita worked her wrists against the restraints, resolving to break free and make a run for it. Better to die trying than sitting helpless in a chair. "What's haunting you, Senator?"

A sad smile formed on his lips. He dragged his gaze back to Rita. "It wasn't long ago that I was young like you. Had a bright, limitless future ahead of me. I was an aspiring politician with big dreams and impossible goals. No money," he sighed. "I accepted a huge endorsement for my campaign with a single string attached. I couldn't allow the docks to be renovated. No one could buy them. No one could rebuild. I had to use my position to keep them as they were. Unused and abandoned. It seemed simple to me. They'd literally asked me to do nothing."

"You had to know that wasn't good," Rita said. "Why would someone give you money for something like that, if not for something nefarious?"

He made a strange face. "It's hard to say now what I was thinking then, before I'd been through so much. Maybe I wanted to believe in easy money. Maybe I wasn't yet jaded. Whatever the reason, I accepted the money and agreed to their terms, moved to Frankfort after the election and forgot about this insignificant little town. The company who'd supported my campaign sent money regularly. It was nice."

"Gray Line," Rita muttered.

The senator's mouth opened. His bushy salt-and-pepper brows crowded together. "Yes. Eventually, curiosity got the best of me, and I pushed for details. When

I saw the guns and realized what I'd done, I demanded more money." He shook his head sadly. "They threatened me. Threatened my family. My career. My world. They said I ought to keep quiet and be thankful they were only moving the guns along the river and not through my state."

Rita continued to struggle with her bindings, fighting through the blinding pain in one shoulder as she worked the rope with her opposite wrist. She only needed to loosen it enough to slip free. "Then Gray Line made a move to buy it themselves."

"By then I'd learned enough to know that if the state sold to them, they'd put up a storage unit and keep their supplies here. The potential income of the operation would triple, plus the problem would no longer be limited to secret river rendezvous. Now, the crime would be on our shores, I wouldn't see any extra cash for it, and if anyone found out, I would be the villain."

"So you had Minsk killed? Why? He was just a middleman."

"He overheard me encouraging the governor about renovating the docks. It's ultimately his call, and I figured if Gray Line wasn't interested in upping my cut, I'd force them out, talk the governor into making good on his campaign promise to revitalize the area. Then Minsk showed up, claiming he had a potential buyer. I knew who he worked for. I had to stop him. What else could I do?"

"You could've gone to the authorities. You should've come clean."

Color torched the senator's face. "Everything's not that simple!" His voice roared through the rickety barn, sending hidden birds into the air. "I could've come clean, and Minsk could've reported it all back to Gray Line or the local media. He could've gotten me killed or revealed me as a traitor to my constituents. I'd facilitated the use of our docks by gunrunners for years."

He balled his hands into fists, looking suddenly heartbroken. "Killing Minsk should've bought me time to figure this out. Instead, you showed up and made everything worse. That thumb drive you stole had years and years of documentation. I know you've already given it to the authorities because you used a fake in the drop today, and the entire sheriff's department was there when the shooting broke out. It stands to reason that the sheriff would have sent it straight to Tech Support. I can't have anyone figuring out Gray Line has been running guns, so I've asked my contact at the FBI to collect the pen for me. He'll claim jurisdiction, and that will clean up the evidence. Except for one problematic eyewitness."

Rita worked harder at the fraying ropes, raking them along the jagged rungs of her chair. "Maybe you and I can make a deal. Let me live, and I'll never say anything about what you've told me. You'll kill me if I do."

"I'm afraid it's far too late for that." He raised two fingers to his mouth and puffed out an earsplitting whistle.

The shooter reappeared in the doorway, backlit by a hazy twilight sky and slowly rising moon.

The elongated shadow of a handgun stretched firmly from one hand.

Chapter Twenty

"Wait!" Rita called out to the senator's retreating figure. "It doesn't have to be like this. Just tell the truth!" She rocked and jerked in her seat, begging her ties to snap and her body to be free. "Come back!"

The senator didn't stop, and he was soon outside the barn.

The shooter moved in front of the chair. "Close your eyes."

Rita's bottom lip quivered and her stubborn chin inched higher. She could see the differences in the fake deputy jacket now. Not to mention that the real thing was worn by a hero. This one was the costume of a monster. She locked eyes with her soon-to-be executioner. She hated the mockery of the uniform all the more, knowing how important it was to Cole and his family. "Why pretend to be a deputy? What's your point? If you're trying to blend in, why not wear something less eye-catching?"

He smiled. "You're wrong, because no one looks twice at law enforcement. I can go anywhere in this jacket, no questions asked. People step aside and don't interrupt."

The distant click of a closing car door swept through the night, followed closely by the gentle purr of an engine. Apparently the senator wasn't staying around for Rita's disposal.

The gunman widened his stance. "Now, close your eyes."

"No."

He rolled his head over one shoulder, then fixed her with an impatient expression. "Look, lady, this isn't personal, but if you cooperate, I promise never to visit your brother again. He can heal up and live his life like this never happened."

Rita stifled a sob. She let her lids drift shut. Her hands fisted at her back, the frayed rope biting into her skin. Her time was up.

"I'm sorry," she whispered, hoping everyone she'd let down could somehow know this wasn't what she'd wanted. She was supposed to watch Ryan grow old. She'd wanted justice for those who were hurt by the senator's selfish and sinister behavior. Most of all, she'd wanted a chance to tell Cole Garrett that she loved him.

Rita imagined Cole's face, his warm smile and the haven of his protective arms as she waited for the end to come.

The gunshot boomed like thunder, ringing in her ears and stealing her breath. Fear radiated through her in bone-crushing shock, but the pain didn't come.

A muted thud lifted her eyelids.

The gunman lay at her feet, a growing puddle of his blood staining his faux deputy jacket.

"Rita!" Cole Garrett limped forward from the open

barn door, one arm in a sling, one foot in a boot cast. "Are you okay?"

She gave the fallen gunman one more look. His unseeing eyes confirmed it. "Yes," she sobbed. She was going to be fine.

A wail of relief rolled through her. "You're hurt!" She rocked on her seat, struggling to free her pinned arms. "How are you here? Are you okay? West said you went to the hospital."

Cole kicked the dead man's gun away, then kneeled at her side.

"I'm fine." The distant drone of sirens grew steadily in the distance. "We traced the call." He cut quickly through her ropes, freeing her wrists, then massaging them gently in his hands.

Rita squeaked from the pressure. Tears ran over her cheeks. One arm hung limply at her side. "It's out of socket," she said, doing her best to be strong for the man who was always strong for her.

"Here." Cole stripped the sling from his shoulder and hooked it over Rita's head. He slid her aching arm into the hammock and adjusted the length of material behind her. "Uncle Henry's already on the way."

Rita cradled her arm in appreciation and relief. "Thank you." She pressed her cheek against his chest and cried.

Cole kissed her head and stroked her hair. "You're safe now, and I won't let anyone or anything hurt you ever again."

Rita held him tight, melding herself to him before she fell apart.

"You were so smart to hide Ryan's phone," he said, nuzzling his cheek against her head. "I don't know what I would've done if I hadn't found you in time."

"I love you," Rita blurted. "I know it's soon and it's silly, but it's true, and whatever you think about that is fine, but I need you to know."

Cole pulled back an inch, a peculiar look in his eye. "Yeah?"

Someone cleared their throat nearby.

Rita looked for the interruption, and discovered West at the barn's entrance, gripping the senator's elbow. The politician's hands were cuffed behind his back.

"I hate to break this up," he said, "but I'm hoping Miss Horn can provide a formal statement about why Senator Sayers was caught racing away from her abduction site."

Cole moved back into her line of sight, successfully blocking out her view of West and everything else. He waved a hand overhead, dismissing his brother. "You said you love me?"

"Very much."

He bent his knees and let loose a rodeo-worthy hoot! He feathered kisses over her nose and cheeks, smiling with every press and release of his lips. "I love you, too."

"You do?"

"Oh, yeah." He looped his good arm over her shoulders and turned her toward the door. "You want to get out of here? Maybe visit a hospital?"

She laughed.

Together they shuffled toward the carousel of red

and white lights flashing in the evening sky. An ambulance pulled up.

"Maybe Uncle Henry can give us a lift," Cole suggested.

"That's fine. As long as I don't have to ride in a trunk."

SNOW AND HOLIDAY music drifted in the air outside Rita's home. Her driveway and half the street were lined with cars in both directions. Cole straightened his jacket before knocking. Thanks to a double shift, he hadn't seen Rita in nearly twenty-four hours, and his chest was already flooded with warmth in anticipation.

She was sure to be smiling tonight. Ryan had finally been released from the recovery center where he'd spent the last three weeks regaining his strength and coordination. According to Rita, he'd already rescheduled his dropped classes for after Christmas break.

Dogged determination was definitely in the Horn genes.

Rita swept her door open, pouring the warm scents of holiday cookies, casseroles and hot chocolate over Cole's senses. She greeted him with a kiss and a smile. "Come in," she urged, tugging his sleeve and nearly vibrating with enthusiasm. "I can't believe how many people are here. I don't even know all these people. I think half of them are named Garrett!"

Cole stole another kiss, then scanned the crowded room. Her neighbors had dibs on the kitchen table, chatting and laughing around steaming mugs and full plates. A few office workers from the municipal building were chatting animatedly in the corner. Ryan and

Nurse Stacy were tucked up close on the couch, a fuzzy cat on each of their laps. A middle-aged man with Rita's eyes spoke animatedly to the couple. "Is that your dad?" Cole asked, downright shocked when she nodded. Her dad had said he was coming home when he'd finally returned her calls, but the only one who'd believed him was Ryan. "Well, I'm glad he came," Cole said, and he meant it.

"Me, too, I think. He says he's going to retire," Rita said. "I'll believe it when I see it, but so far, he seems to be trying to make up for lost time. He even apologized for not choosing us over duty more often. I liked hearing that."

"I bet you did." Cole slung an arm over her shoulders and kissed her head. "I will always choose you."

Rita smiled, and the room grew brighter.

Cole gave the crowd another long look. Rita was right, the other fifteen or so people were Garretts. Cole had personally invited them to come.

"They all showed up to welcome Ryan home," she said. "Can you believe it?" She pressed a palm to her heart. "Is this what it's like to have a big family? Because I love it. Your dad invited Ryan to go bass fishing. Your mom brought so much food I won't have to cook for a week." She wiped the pad of one thumb under each eye. "I miss my mom so much it hurts."

"I know." Christmas was a rough season to be alone, but if things went Cole's way today, Rita would never be short on family again. He wrapped her in his arms and smoothed a hand over the length of her hair, marveling at how this one woman had so irrevocably changed his life.

"There you are." West's voice boomed through the room. He left a kiss on his wife's forehead, then wove a path to Cole's side. "Time for those announcements?"

Rita furrowed her narrow brow. "Announcements? Do you have news about the senator?"

"Attention!" West tapped his fork against his little plate. "I have some news that many of you will enjoy hearing. I know I did."

Slowly, the room quieted. A sea of expectant eyes turned in West's direction.

"First of all," he began, "I want to thank Rita for opening up her home to all of us. Given what she's been through, some folks might be inclined to never open their door again."

The crowd chuckled.

"And speaking of men I wouldn't invite inside," West continued, "I received news today that Senator Sayers is in jail awaiting trial without bail. The state believes they've got enough evidence to put him away for a long while." He turned his attention directly to Rita. "It seems the thumb drive you delivered into my hands has provided the ATF with everything they needed to make multiple arrests within Gray Line Enterprises, a known gun-trafficking organization that they've been watching for more than two years. My big brother Blake was able to use your tip that someone from the FBI would try to collect the drive from Tech Support, and that guy was arrested, as well."

Rita beamed. "You're kidding."

Cole began a slow clap that rolled through the room.

Her brother pounded his hands together and chanted her name.

Cole grinned.

Ryan had admitted to taking her truck after being told not to for a bunch of little brother reasons. One, he only needed it to make one trip, so what could go wrong? Two, she hadn't moved it from the lot where he'd left it at his school, so she obviously didn't need it back right away. And, three, he couldn't reach her by phone to beg some more, because unbeknownst to him, her phone was in the river by that time.

West extended a hand in her direction for a formal shake.

Rita accepted. "Thank you."

Isla, from the mayor's office, was next to make a scene. "I've got something, too," she hollered, sliding to the front of the crowd. "The mayor announced today that the governor is taking control of all monies seized from the senator's business with Gray Line and reallocating the funds to reclaim the docks!"

Rita's jaw dropped.

"There's more." Isla beamed, clearly enjoying her moment in the spotlight. "He was so moved by your love for those stray cats that he vowed the first business opened there will be an animal shelter."

Rita's eyes glistened. "That's amazing! Thank you."

Isla gave the crowd another smile, then sashayed away looking quite proud of herself.

Rita turned to Cole with a look of sheer joy.

Cole's heart thundered in his chest. The announcements were made. Rita was happy. Now, there was only one thing left to do.

"Rita Horn," he began, a ridiculous quiver wiggling in his chest. "Knowing you has changed my life, my world and my dreams."

West tapped his fork against his plate. "It's happening."

Cole ignored him and pressed on, retrieving a small gold band from his pocket. He looked into Rita's wide hazel eyes, then slowly he lowered onto one knee.

Rita's head began to nod in agreement.

"Now wait." Cole smiled, his chest tight with elation. "I haven't asked you anything yet."

"Yes."

Everyone laughed, and Rita's gaze jumped toward the crowd.

Ryan lifted a slow thumbs-up to his sister.

She turned back to Cole with tear-filled eyes. "Yes."

Cole gathered her trembling hands in his. "I realize we haven't known each other long, but I'd like to know you forever."

Fat tears spilled over her cheeks. "Yes."

He stood and offered her his handkerchief. "Marry me," he said.

Rita rose onto her toes and planted her lips to his in a shameless display of love and desire.

The crowd erupted in cheers of utter delight, but Cole was certain there would never be a happier man alive than him in that very moment.

* * * * *

Look for the next book in Julie Anne Lindsey's
Garrett Valor miniseries in February.

And don't miss the previous titles in the series:

Federal Agent Under Fire
The Sheriff's Secret

Available now from Harlequin Intrigue!

Franklin County, Tennessee
Monday, February 25, 9:10 p.m.

The red-and-blue lights flashed in the night.

Audrey Anderson opened her car door and stepped out
onto the gravel road. She grimaced and wished she'd taken
time to change her shoes, but time was not an available luxury
when the police scanner spit out the code for a shooting that
ended in a call to the coroner. Good thing her dedicated editor,
Brian Peterson, had his ear to the police radio pretty much
24/7 and immediately texted her.

The sheriff's truck was already on-site, along with two
county cruisers and the coroner's van. So far no news vans
and no cars that she noticed belonging to other reporters
from the tri-county area. Strange, that cocky reporter from
the *Tullahoma Telegraph* almost always arrived on the scene
before Audrey. Maybe she had a friend in the department.

Then again, Audrey had her own sources, too. She reached
back into the car for her bag. So far the closest private source
she had was the sheriff himself—which was only because he
still felt guilty for cheating on her back in high school.

Audrey was not above using that guilt whenever the need
arose.

HIEXP0119

Tonight seemed like the perfect time to remind the man she'd once thought she would marry that he owed her one or two or a hundred.

She shuddered as the cold night air sent a shiver through her. Late February was marked by all sorts of lovely blooms and promises of spring, but it was all just an illusion. It was still winter and Mother Nature loved letting folks know who was boss. Like tonight—the gorgeous sixty-two-degree sunny day had turned into a bone-chilling evening. Audrey shivered, wishing she'd worn a coat to dinner.

Buncombe Road snaked through a farming community situated about halfway between Huntland and Winchester— every agricultural mile fell under the Franklin County sheriff's jurisdiction. The houses, mostly farmhouses sitting amid dozens if not hundreds of acres of pastures and fields, were scattered few and far between. But that wasn't the surprising part of the location. This particular house and farm belonged to a Mennonite family. Rarely did violence or any other sort of trouble within this quiet, closed community ripple beyond its boundaries. Most issues were handled privately and silently. The Mennonites kept to themselves for the most part and never bothered anyone. A few operated public businesses within the local community, and most interactions were kept strictly within the business domain. There was no real intermingling or socializing within the larger community— not even Winchester, which was the county seat and buzzed with activity.

Whatever happened inside this turn-of-the-nineteenth-century farmhouse tonight was beyond the closed community's ability to settle amid their own ranks.

Don't miss
In Self Defense *by Debra Webb,*
available February 2019 wherever
Harlequin® Intrigue books and ebooks are sold.

www.Harlequin.com

Love Harlequin romance?

DISCOVER.

Be the first to find out about promotions, news and exclusive content!

Facebook.com/HarlequinBooks

Twitter.com/HarlequinBooks

Instagram.com/HarlequinBooks

Pinterest.com/HarlequinBooks

ReaderService.com

EXPLORE.

Sign up for the Harlequin e-newsletter and download a free book from any series at **TryHarlequin.com.**

CONNECT.

Join our Harlequin community to share your thoughts and connect with other romance readers!
Facebook.com/groups/HarlequinConnection

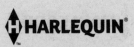

HARLEQUIN®

ROMANCE WHEN YOU NEED IT

HSOCIAL2018